EBURY PRESS

SOUFFLÉ

Anand Ranganathan is a scientist and an author. He has written three novels: *The Land of the Wilted Rose* (Rupa, 2012), *For Love and Honour* (Bloomsbury, 2015) and *The Rat Eater* (Bloomsbury, 2019; co-authored). His forthcoming book is on India's forgotten scientists (Penguin, 2023; co-authored).

ADVANCE PRAISE FOR THE BOOK

'If this psychological, compelling and unpredictable novel doesn't keep you hooked, give up reading'—Ashwin Sanghi, author

'*Soufflé* is a literary thriller with enough twists and turns to leave you breathless. A brilliant page-turner from a master storyteller'—Amish Tripathi, author

Soufflé

ANAND RANGANATHAN

EBURY
PRESS

An imprint of Penguin Random House

EBURY PRESS

USA | Canada | UK | Ireland | Australia
New Zealand | India | South Africa | China

Ebury Press is part of the Penguin Random House group of companies
whose addresses can be found at global.penguinrandomhouse.com

Published by Penguin Random House India Pvt. Ltd
4th Floor, Capital Tower 1, MG Road,
Gurugram 122 002, Haryana, India

First published in Ebury Press by Penguin Random House India 2023

ISBN 9780143459408

Typeset in Requiem by MAP Systems, Bengaluru, India

www.penguin.co.in

I

The night is still except for the sonorous lapping of the waves against the ramparts of the Lake Palace Hotel. One stronger than usual surge upsets a peacock, making it gather its spread and take flight from the overhanging eave of a canopy. It glides clumsily across the lawns and settles by the French window of the hotel's flagship restaurant. Inside, beautiful people are conversing at candlelit tables, in a setting reminiscent of the Rajwada. Waiters hustle across the floor, catering to the guests' every need. A live *jugalbandi* of *morchang*, *khadtal* and *sarangi* adds to the ambience. On one of the tables by the window—the house peacock now trotting and nibbling the other side of it—sits Abhishek Sehgal, a handsome man in his late thirties. Opposite him, fiddling with her pearl necklace, is the bewitching Nayantara, also in her thirties. A waiter in crisp jodhpurs steps up to pluck Dom Perignon from the ice bucket and upon receiving a gentle nod, replenishes the flutes. A second server arrives with the dessert and arranges the plates before the two guests, realigning the spoons as a matter of habit. Both soon retreat, bowing their heads.

Abhishek notices the monogrammed plate. It carries his initials. He glances nervously at Nayantara. Oblivious to his stare, she is focused on her dessert, the signature soufflé. With the first spoon itself, her eyes close in ecstasy. As she whimpers in delight, Abhishek types a quick text on his phone. 'So far so good.'

Across the hall, veiled by an ornate Kota *jaali*, the Michelin-star chef responds to Abhishek's text with a 'thumbs up' emoji.

Abhishek smiles at the reply and glances up. He is horror-struck. Nayantara is already done with her dessert and is licking the spoon. Her face bears the look of having attained nirvana. She opens her eyes slowly, as though in a daze, and smiles at him. But her smile turns to bewilderment as she sees Abhishek tear away his napkin and rush over. The commotion makes the other guests curious. The music stops abruptly. So does the clinking of cutlery. Waiters freeze where they are and turn their stares to the table. The Michelin-star chef emerges from behind the screen and bounds across the hall, in time to witness Abhishek grab Nayantara from behind and squeeze her waist. Nayantara shrieks as she is hoisted in the air. A crowd collects. Chaos ensues.

Motorboat sirens wail as Nayantara is rushed to a hospital. The chef accompanying her and Abhishek tries to comfort them, but is upset and jumpy himself. At the ghat, an ambulance is waiting. Nayantara is placed on a stretcher. Abhishek and the chef hop aboard. Soon the ambulance is negotiating the crowded city streets, its siren blaring.

The *Aravali General Hospital* emergency room, normally buzzing with activity, is cloaked in nervous silence. One can even hear the shudder of the wall clock's hands as they jerk forward. Abhishek, his head in his hands, is staring at the tall bottle of Dulcolax on the table opposite. An hour and an age of anxiety later, the anteroom doors swing open and the doctor strides out. He reassures Abhishek and the chef. They nod in relief. Silence ensues once more, but is shortly broken by the gurgle of the toilet flush. Nayantara soon emerges, escorted by a female nurse. Nayantara is visibly drained. She lurches forward and stumbles, latching on to the edge of a table for support. She stares at Abhishek and opens her palm slowly, to reveal a diamond ring. The solitaire dazzles as it catches the light. Abhishek rushes to embrace Nayantara even as the chef extricates himself from the lounge sofa and approaches the couple. 'Hiding the ring in the soufflé was his idea,' he tells Nayantara with an uneasy grin, pointing an accusatory finger at Abhishek. 'I am so sorry for all this. Really am.'

Nayantara's weary face breaks into a mischievous smile. 'One whole hour,' she complains, 'One whole bloody hour. My knees are aching like hell with all that squatting.' Glancing at Abhishek, she adds, 'The doctor insisted I use the Indian toilet and not the WC, in case the ring dropped out and disappeared down the hole.'

The chef is struggling to contain his laughter. 'All is well that ends well. Guys, I need to rush now, or the same fate awaits me. And it won't be a million-dollar diamond ring that slops out of me once they are done torturing me, I assure you.'

Nayantara titters, and a second later sucks in a groan as the price of the ring registers. She narrows her eyes at Abhishek, and Abhishek at the chef, who is embarrassed at having blurted out the price.

'Sorry about that,' says the chef to Nayantara. 'I wasn't supposed to disclose the price—Abhishek had extracted a promise from me.'

Abhishek blushes. Nayantara giggles, holding the ring. 'And look what got extracted from *me*.'

Abhishek and the chef join in the laughter. 'Listen, I must get going,' says the chef, 'And Tara, sorry again.'

'Don't be silly,' scoffs Nayantara. 'Thank you for everything. And that soufflé—what can I say.'

'But it didn't do the trick, did it,' laments Abhishek.

'Well, all you have to do to find out, Abhishek, is to drop down on your knee,' quips Nayantara.

Abhishek smiles. Egged on by the chef, he goes down on one knee, and taking Nayantara's hand, asks her, 'Will you marry me, Tara?'

'Yes,' says Nayantara pretending sheepishness. The room erupts in applause and cheers as the chef exits, waving his goodbyes.

The taxi carrying the chef zips through Udaipur's streets. Arriving at the airport, it veers into a side entrance, leaving in its wake a cloud of dust. Stunned security guards stare after it and, outraged, are about to chase the car when they realize the occupant must be a VIP for the taxi to have even dared the manoeuvre. And sure enough, they find their superior tailing the taxi in his open jeep, all the way to a private jet that is ready and waiting on the tarmac. The chef climbs out of the taxi and jogs up the retractable ladder. A minute later, sipping his drink, he is admiring the unrivalled splendour as the plane flies over the Lake Palace Hotel. The chef leans back again and sinks into the leather seat with a lingering sigh. The cabin hum is comforting, a lullaby. Sleep beckons. But a stewardess soon arrives with a plate of culinary delights. She mumbles a few pleasantries and requests an autograph, that the chef obliges, a trifle irritated. Sipping his drink, he glances around distractedly. On his left is a shelf stocked with magazines and books. The book on top bears his portrait. It is titled *Sweet & Sour, my journey from Mumtaz Sarai to Michelin Star—Rajiv Mehra*.

Rajiv stares at the cover—that piercing yet soft look, chiselled features, day-old stubble and the famous grin. He turns away, scratching his beard, bored. Picking up the remote, he switches on the screen in front of him and settles on a food channel. Try as he might, he can't escape himself. There he is, along with three other Michelin-star chefs, holding forth in a *MaestroChef special*. Rajiv and the irascible Gilbert Ramsay are pretending to indulge in a fight over the ingredients of an Indian dish as the audience cheers and hoots. Rajiv bookends Gilbert's face with two slices of bread and screams, 'What are you! Tell me, what are you?' The audience answers for Gilbert, 'An idiot sandwich!' and the house erupts in mirth.

Rajiv switches off the screen and settles back in his reclined seat, covering his eyes with a sleep mask. His day has just begun; he might as well catch a wink or two.

* * *

The wheels screech as they meet the scorched tarmac of the Dubai international airport. The plane taxis to the area reserved for private jets. As the hatch peels down, a helicopter in the vicinity guns to power. Rajiv, a shimmering figure in the heat emanating from the tarmac, breathes in the warm Dubai air and stretches his arms and legs. He is met by a team that ushers him straight to the waiting chopper, and soon they are in the skies

over Dubai, flying past its twinkling and glimmering buildings.
Dawn is breaking as, ten minutes later, the chopper descends to
land atop Burj Al Arab. Rajiv spots the hotel manager Ermanno
Meazza among the men waiting below on the helipad, as they
scamper to avoid the whirlpool of wind and dust.

'Welcome to Burj, Mr Mehra,' shouts Ermanno over the
enormous din of the blades.

'Thank you,' says Rajiv. 'I am sorry I got delayed but it was
an emergency.'

'I am told it was,' chuckles Ermanno, as the two walk away
from the chopper. 'I hope Mr and Mrs Sehgal choose Burj for
their honeymoon.'

Rajiv is in no mood for small talk. 'What time is the crown
prince entertaining Mr Patel for brunch?' he asks curtly.

'11.00 a.m., sir. The Indian embassy reconfirmed. So did
His Excellency Ahmed Al Maktoum's office. But nothing to
worry. We have an hour at hand. And I have already passed on
your detailed instructions to the team.'

'Good. Take me straight to the kitchen,' says Rajiv as they
stride through the bay area to the lift lobby.

Rajiv enters the spacious kitchen to rapturous applause.
His regiment, that includes two Michelin-star chefs,
appears all set for the battle ahead. Rajiv jumps straight into
commanding them, shouting instructions, tasting the dishes
that have been prepared during the mock drill. He guides
them into combat, never letting their attention waver, keeping
them on their toes even as he rushes about the expanse of the
kitchen. Plans fall into place like jigsaw pieces and before one
knows it, an exquisite Indian platter crowns the dining table
across which the Dubai and Gujarat delegations are seated in
the Royal Hall of Nations.

'I haven't had such good food in decades, your Excellency,' beams the chief minister of Gujarat. 'And to top it all, this is Indian cuisine. I am ashamed.'

The crown prince gathers his flowing satin *kandora* and produces a knowing smile. 'Wait till you try the masterpiece, Mr Chief Minister.'

As though on cue, arrives the signature soufflé.

The chief minister takes a spoonful, allows it to acclimatize inside his mouth, and then lets it slip gently down his palate. A sigh escapes his lips. His eyes close. A moment later they open in astonishment. He is lost for words.

'I told you so,' gloats the crown prince. 'I don't call it a masterpiece for nothing.'

'How? How is this possible?' exclaims the chief minister. 'Your Excellency, forget the ten-billion-dollar investment we have just signed an MoU for; I will double it if you tell me the secret recipe.'

The crown prince throws his head back and laughs. 'First things first, Mr Chief Minister. So, what is the main ingredient?'

Mr Patel mulls over his response, taking in another spoonful. 'Dates? Apricot?' he answers, unsure.

'It is, what do you call it, yes—apple gourd. Tinda!' chortles the crown prince.

The chief minister lets out a loud 'No'. He repeats it, shaking his head.

'Tinda soufflé,' declares the crown prince grandly. 'And made by none other than—' He turns to his secretary, and the doors sweep open to let Rajiv in.

'Meet Rajiv Mehra, Mr Chief Minister. The greatest living chef in the world,' declares the crown prince.

The chief minister greets Rajiv warmly. 'Join my delegation, Mr Mehra,' he jokes. 'Together we can conquer the world.'

'Too late,' chides the crown prince, 'Rajiv is in my army. And together we are already conquering the world. One dish at a time.'

An hour later, Rajiv is back inside a private jet, fast asleep, mask covering his eyes. He is returning to India. On the adjacent seat is a magazine, its cover showing Rajiv's smiling face with the caption 'A Single Dish'.

* * *

A limousine is waiting on the tarmac when the plane touches down in Mumbai. It drives Rajiv to his home in Pali Hill, a spacious, airy flat, sparsely and tastefully done up. Rajiv turns on the TV and runs the bath. The sound of sloshing water coming from the bathroom mixes with the news on TV. India's richest man, and the world's ninth richest, is celebrating his birthday today. Felicitations are pouring in from film stars and politicians and business tycoons. The segment shows footage of his skyscraper Mumbai home, outside which there is a line of luxury cars, with superstars and luminaries disembarking, bouquets in hand. Before entering the building, the celebrities pose momentarily in front of a wall of roses—till they are politely pushed along the raised platform by the next in the assembly line. The horde of reporters asks them for any chatter or gossip regarding the eagerly anticipated birthday bash slated for tonight. Rumours are it is going to be held at the iconic Taaj Grand, for which the entire hotel has been booked. The scene shifts to outside the Taaj, where already a considerable crowd of reporters has assembled, as guests arrive from all around the world. From Hillary Clinton to Tom Cruise to Bill Gates to Roger Federer, the who's who of the world have descended to celebrate Mihir Kothari's sixtieth birthday. The security surrounding the Taaj befits a prime minister or a president, informs the reporter, just before his cameraman is shoved aside by the thickset palm of a bouncer.

Rajiv emerges from the bathroom rubbing his hair with a towel, with a second one wrapped around his waist. He ambles into his wardrobe and eyes the collection of shirts and jackets, picking out a light blue combination. Dressed, he flicks the TV off and exits, carrying a duffle bag with him. Downstairs, a Mercedes belonging to the Taaj is waiting to ferry him to the hotel. Rajiv requests the chauffeur to make a brief stop at Dalal Street even as he gets busy on his phone, shouting instructions to his team. The instructions carry on for a good fifteen minutes. At the other end, having put their phones on speaker, is Rajiv's trusted battalion, taking down notes, some even recording Rajiv. What will go into the making of the dishes is narrated in exquisite detail, from the exact amount of each ingredient to the duration of its preparation, in seconds not minutes. And the fact that Rajiv is rattling all this out from memory never fails to astound his team.

Three traffic jams, two call-drops and five-recipe instructions later, the chauffeur informs Rajiv that they have reached the *mantralaya*. 'To hell with this jam, I'll walk from here,' says Rajiv, disembarking at the mouth of Dalal Street. The crowd of office-going pedestrians is building up but is not intimidating yet; in fact, it's quite a pleasant walk. The meandering lane behind the stock exchange takes Rajiv to an old Parsi shop famous for its Gujarati snacks. It has a section that serves tea and rusk and is currently bustling with customers. The owner, a portly old man wearing the trademark *pheta*, greets Rajiv affectionately. He reaches below the counter for a package and rests it gently on top. 'Fresh theplas. Made this morning. Just how you asked,' he tells Rajiv. On the wall behind him is a garlanded portrait of Mohanbhai Kothari, the patriarch of the Kothari dynasty. The *dhoop* in front of it billows smoky fragrance. Rajiv picks up the package and thanks the owner and departs. Back inside the car, he tells the chauffeur to take him to the Taaj.

The Mercedes enters the Taaj from the rear gate, which is empty of reporters and the razzmatazz. Almost. One enterprising journalist materializes out of thin air, and before Rajiv can weave and duck away, a mic is thrust in front of his face.

'Sir, one comment. Just one,' squeaks the reporter, now almost jogging beside Rajiv.

'Not now, please,' says Rajiv affably.

But the reporter is having none of it. 'Sir, you have known Mr Kothari for close to a decade now. You are his family friend. Together with Manish Kalra, you were tasked with organizing the marriage celebrations of Mr Kothari's son just recently, in fact a month ago. They still talk of the feast, so grand it was. All I want to ask is, will tonight's dinner be any different?'

'Every dinner is different,' says Rajiv hurriedly, trying to brush the reporter off.

'Sir, one last question,' insists the reporter, 'Sir, we have heard Mr Kothari employs a dozen tasters who taste everything that is served to him, at home or at restaurants or parties, but whenever you prepare his food, he insists that only you taste it beforehand. Is this true?'

Rajiv is startled at the reporter's knowledge of this fact. 'Yes, it is. As they say, the devil must get a taste of his own brew,' he jokes, taking longer strides so as to leave the reporter behind, which at long last he manages to.

The hotel manager is waiting in the lobby. He greets Rajiv enthusiastically and escorts him to his suite on the fourth floor. Rajiv dumps his duffle on the bed, changes into his chef's gear—arranged thoughtfully on the table for him—and asks the manager to take him straight to where he is going to spend the rest of the day.

* * *

The aluminium panelled-double doors of the Taaj kitchen swing open to reveal a waiting army. This is Dubai redux, but multiple levels up. The welcoming done, the speeches made, Rajiv gets down to business, manoeuvring his men expertly, readying what is going to be a seven-course meal in honour of Mihir Kothari. The media has billed it as the Seven Wonders of the World and talked of its elements endlessly for days. Senior chefs hurry about yelling directions and an entourage of junior chefs and attendants scurry with heavy loads of pots and pans, even as Rajiv paces the length and breadth of the kitchen, scrutinizing the dishes with an eagle eye, tasting the stocks, instructing the battery of chefs. Everything is leading up to an unforgettable evening.

Amid the noise and the racket, the evening arrives. The hectic, bazaar-like vitality hasn't slackened one bit. Rajiv has been on the floor for the better part of five hours but to look at him, he has just emerged from a shower, ready to take on whatever the day throws at him. His energy is astounding, and it's clearly rubbing off on his supporting staff. Nearly. 'What the hell is that, Emanuele?' he cries all of a sudden. Emanuele Tardelli, the Italian Michelin-star chef, bends down to inspect what has upset Rajiv. He spots it. The trimming of a rose petal in the third storey of the centrepiece birthday cake. The buttercream-frosted petal is off its intended symmetry by a millimetre. '*Mannaggia a me!*' exclaims Emanuele, nodding his wonderment at Rajiv's eagle eye. He crouches further to correct the petal with a pair of tweezers. Rajiv smiles. The rose is perfect now.

* * *

'Shift the rose to near the clavicle, na, uncle,' pleads Subhadra, pirouetting before the mirror. The train of her evening gown whooshes over Manish Kalra's supple frame. 'Easy now,' he cautions, nearly tipping over. He is down on his haunches pinning the dress into shape, his mouth supplying the pins as and when he needs them.

'The rose isn't going anywhere. And certainly not to the clavicle, Ms Subhadra Kothari,' he says.

Subhadra clicks her tongue and looks despondently at her aunt Neelima, reposing on the Barcelona a few feet away. 'Tell him, na, Fai! He listens only to you.'

Neelima looks up from her *Harper's* and gives Subhadra a quick once-over. 'Give the kid what she wants, Manish,' she says lazily, returning to her magazine. 'Stop being a bore. *Bacchiyon se bhi ladoge ab?*'

'No,' insists Manish even as he takes another pin from between his lips and arranges the swathe of sequinned velvet over Subhadra's hips. 'The rose is always positioned where the brooch is pinned. It's not travelling up, all right, darling? Final.'

'Sorry, Subs. I tried,' says Neelima, tossing the magazine away.

Manish straightens. Grabbing Subhadra by her shoulders, he stares hard at her in the mirror, positioning her torso just how he wants it. 'Perfecto,' he exults, pushing Subhadra away playfully. 'Off you go girl.'

'About time, too,' sighs Neelima. 'Two bloody hours. You are getting old, Manish.'

Manish rolls his eyes. 'Your turn now, honey.'

'What, me?'

'Time to turn you into a princess. Aren't you tired of looking like a queen all the time?'

'There's an age for every dress.'

'And I have a dress for every age.'

'Talk of backhanded compliments,' says Neelima, throwing the magazine at Manish.

'Seriously, N.'

'Stop it, Manish. I am all right in this evening dress.'

'Come off it. You look like Edwina Mountbatten.'

'Are you saying Krishen is Louis—or Nehru?'

'Churchill if you ask me.'

Neelima throws her head back and laughs. 'You are getting better at this, M.'

'Achcha enough *bakwas*. Come na. Let me transform you.'

'I am all right in my Versace, thank you.'

'The cowl drape is so last century, hon.'

'Well, *I* am so last century.'

'Uff.'

'Enough,' says Neelima. 'Subs, it's time to leave. Now be a nice girl and blow a kiss to Manish uncle for all his troubles. Careful there, babes, don't bend too much or your dress might rip.'

'Very funny,' says Subhadra.

'Turrah, you two,' snorts Manish, twiddling his fingers.

Inside the stretch limo, engaged to accommodate Subhadra and her meandering gown, Neelima sinks into the leather and lets out a tired breath. 'Two hours, Subs,' she complains, but then quickly punctuates her irritation with a compliment. 'Worth it. You look magnificent.'

'Thanks, Fai,' says Subhadra, correcting the fall of her gown. Her phone comes to life. It is Vrinda Kothari, Subhadra's mother-in-law. 'I can't talk now, Ma,' she tells her, 'I can't even pick the phone up; my dress will be ruined.' But Vrinda is in no mood to give in. 'Put me on the video screen. It's important,' she commands. Subhadra relents. A moment later, Vrinda's mother-in-law Miraben appears on the screen together with her. They are fiddling with the phone, not sure how to handle the video call. 'Quick, Ma,' cries Subhadra, as Neelima stares at the screen shaking her head. She knows what this is about.

'This is Mahapatra's latest. How am I looking?' asks Vrinda. She wants an opinion on her choker. It is studded with hundreds of diamonds and emeralds and traps every bit of light that comes its way. The jewellery designer Arindam Mahapatra enters the frame from the side, looking sheepish.

Neelima can't resist. 'Oh god, Vrinda. Mahapatra has turned you into Cleopatra.'

'Quiet!'

'It's ridiculous. I can't see your face, your neck has been set on fire.'

'Don't listen to Neelima on this, Vrinda. She's just jealous.' The owner of this remark now comes into view. It is Neelima's mother and the matriarch of the Kothari clan, Miraben Kothari.

'As though Cleopatra wasn't enough, here comes Queen Elizabeth,' sniggers Neelima. 'Ma, what's up with you two? If she's wearing a nuclear reactor, you're wearing a dog cone.'

Miraben snatches the phone from Vrinda and toys with it, claiming it's ringing. It actually is. She says a curt goodbye to Subhadra and Neelima and disconnects, switching to the other caller. It is Viramani, personal secretary to the Kothari brothers Mihir and Rupesh. 'Bolo, Vir,' says Miraben in a rushed tone.

Vir is a little flustered. He was expecting Vrinda at the other end and not the stern and hard-hearted Miraben. He collects his wits hastily. 'Hello, ma'am,' he mumbles, 'Mihir sir has asked me to inform you and Vrinda ma'am that he is running a little late and will reach the Taaj directly, along with Rupesh sir. There isn't time to come home first.'

Miraben grunts and disconnects the call, leaving Viramani perplexed. He jerks back to life eventually and slips back inside the boardroom where a presentation is in progress. Drifting stealthily along the wall, he arrives to stand behind Mihir. He waits for the opportune moment and crouches down to deliver the message in his master's ear. Mihir nods and shuffles in his chair.

A Chinese man is speaking. Nudging Rupesh, Mihir queries his brother. 'What's your opinion on this 5G technology? That last slide was quite revealing,' he whispers. Rupesh is taken aback, both by the question as well as by being asked it. He thought he'd get through the entire meeting by indulging in WhatsApp and no one would pay any attention. He stutters and gropes for a response. 'I'll have to look into it in more detail,' he says and then quickly changes the topic. 'What time are we leaving for the Taaj?' he asks. Mihir smiles and tilts back to his preferred posture, picking up a cookie from the platter in front of him.

* * *

A steward dressed in coat-tails collects a platter and hurries out of the kitchen, balancing it on the crook of his arm, which already has on it another platter of exquisitely arranged hors d'oeuvres. Waiters and stewards scramble about. Reaching the end of the spacious corridor, the steward twists and with a thrust of his hip swings open the art deco doors of the ballroom. It transports one to another world altogether.

The century-old Taaj ballroom is a sight to behold. The theme is Raj glory, and everything, from the chandeliers to the curtains to the seating to the tables to the linen, is reminiscent of the days of the Raj. The only thing missing is the elephants. The hall, which can accommodate seventy round tables, is packed to capacity, with each table possessing the collective GDP of a small nation.

A hush descends over the ballroom as the Kotharis make an entrance. Guests rush over to greet them; it is as though the crowd is arranging itself around the family. Soon the Kotharis disperse, taking their preferred appendages with them as they drift. Mihir and Rupesh suck away the tycoons; Miraben and Vrinda pull to the side the Bollywood divas and the designers; Subhadra and Rohan draw the scions of the Mumbai dynasties and all future billionaires; and Neelima lures away the working professionals and magazine editors; *National Geographic*, *Vogue* and all that is in between. Hustle and bustle return to the ballroom. Couples dance to live jazz music. Champagne glasses are tolled with forks, speeches are delivered and the cake is cut.

The Kothari table is noisy, with the younger members of the clan egging Mihir to render a romantic number. He refuses politely, to friendly boos. 'Ah, just in time,' he smiles, relieved, as the dessert makes its way to the table.

It is the signature soufflé. Mihir gazes at it in admiration. He has had it numerous times before, but every new occasion feels like the first time. He asks for Rajiv's whereabouts but knows the answer even before it is supplied to him. Rajiv never appears in public at a function he is in charge of. Like a fashion designer or a film director, he prefers to observe the unfolding of his creative masterpiece from a distance, which in fact he is doing presently, watching, unknown to his admirers, their every move, hidden away behind the thick velvet curtains by the orchestra dais. Mihir raises his glass to the absent Rajiv. 'To Rajiv,' he says out loud. 'To Rajiv,' echoes the ballroom. Mihir skims his spoon gently over the soufflé and gathers a spoonful. He raises it to his lips, pauses, draws in a whiff and then places it in his mouth.

Others around the table follow suit. Spoons clink and clank on the crockery. The table resounds with appreciative moans and exclamations. The Kotharis have stopped looking at each other or conversing; it is as though an animal instinct has taken over. Rajiv smiles from afar, observing their behaviour. His gaze lingers on Mihir Kothari, perched on his chair ramrod straight as is his habit, with his hand holding the dessert spoon just above the plate. But there is something peculiar about him. His face is expressionless, his body stiff. His eyes are wide open, unblinking, staring into the distance. A froth of blood is seeping through his compressed lips. It is as though he has gone into rigor mortis. He is dead.

Loud shrieks relay around the ballroom. Guests jerk up from their seats and hurry to the Kothari table. Mihir is gently positioned on the ground, and panicky family members attempt to resuscitate him. Someone cries for a doctor, someone else shouts for everyone to stop having the soufflé. A doctor who is a guest rushes over to examine Mihir and having done so, raises his head and shakes it inconsolably. 'Cyanide poisoning,' he murmurs, barely able to speak. A second passes. Then another. No one is sure what to say, how to react. They begin to look in all directions. Someone spots Rajiv emerging from behind the curtain and cries out, half in disbelief, half accusatory. The lights are still dim, and guests are having trouble identifying him or placing him in the present context. But Rajiv understands. He freezes. A burly security guard grabs his arm. A guest tells him not to. A heated conversation follows. The hotel's medical and ambulance staff arrives, followed soon by the police. The inspector asks Rajiv to accompany him—not a word has escaped Rajiv's lips yet. He nods sluggishly. They exit the ballroom. Outside, the crowd hushes itself at the sight of Rajiv. It is as though Rajiv and the policemen are slicing through a funeral gathering.

'Where are you taking me?' asks Rajiv as they reach the lift foyer. It is difficult to make out the inspector, leave alone the shapes in the crowd, because of the soft and diffused lighting. The entire lobby, including the foyer and the corridors, are candlelit for tonight, like someone is remaking Kubrick's *Barry Lyndon*, scene by scene.

'The police station, first,' replies Inspector Apte narrowing his eyes, also irritated by the lack of proper lighting.

Rajiv nods. 'In which case, can I take my night-time medicines and insulin injections from my room?'

Inspector Apte nods his approval. 'Okay,' he tells Rajiv.

Rajiv points to the lift. 'Thank you. Fourth floor. Maharaja suite.'

The short journey is made in silence, with a policeman clasping tight Rajiv's right hand. On the fourth floor, he leads the policemen through the corridor to the Maharaja suite. A swipe of the card over the lock-handle of the room grants him entry. The duffle bag is lying on the bed. He rummages through it, then turns around to face the inspector. 'The medicines are in the toilet. Can I, please?'

'Be quick,' nods Inspector Apte and crashes on to the sofa. His colleagues, awed by the splendour of their surroundings, follow suit.

Rajiv enters the toilet and locks it from the inside. He moves swiftly down the anteroom, to where the bathtub is. A man is lying curled up in the bath, groaning, barely conscious. It is Rajiv Mehra. The man standing over him reaches his hand up to his face and peels off a hyper-real latex mask mimicking Rajiv's face. He crumples it and stuffs it inside the backpack he has grabbed from above the washbasin. In the same motion, he pulls out a Rolex Submariner with its distinctive blue dial and slips it on his wrist. Time is running out.

He props Rajiv up in the bathtub and removes his belt. Shaping it into a lasso, he slips the noose end over Rajiv's head and tightens it around his neck. He fastens the other end to the door handle. He takes out a bottle of sleeping pills from his backpack, spills some tablets on the floor and some in the basin and places the open bottle by the bathtub. Next, he removes the wrapping from a razor blade, crouches to shift Rajiv to his side, and slits Rajiv's wrist, tossing the blade into the tub. Slinging the backpack over his shoulder, he tiptoes out of the bathroom, leaving Rajiv mumbling incoherently. Walking over to the large window in the anteroom, the man opens it and climbs out, sliding shut the window behind him.

Outside, in the Maharaja suite, Inspector Apte and his colleagues are getting restless. Apte consults his watch and gestures for his colleagues to act. One of them walks up to the toilet and knocks. There is no response. He tries the door handle. It is locked. He shoves at it with his shoulder. The others join him. They are now in a panic. After a few tries, they force open the door, falling and crashing on to the floor with their momentum. The anteroom is empty. They rush to the bathroom. Rajiv is gurgling and frothing at the mouth, his eyelids are jerking open and shut. Blood is oozing out from the slit on his wrist. With every movement of his head, the noose tightens around his neck, making him froth more. Shouting and cursing, the policemen undo the noose carefully and grab Rajiv under his arms and lift him out of the bathtub. They lay him down on the floor and call for assistance, slapping Rajiv's cheeks every now and then to bring him to his senses.

The crowd in the lobby, which has built up steadily over the last half hour, parts as Rajiv is stretchered away. An oxygen mask has been fixed over his face and a drip is being administered, the ambulance attendant holding the pouch up and running alongside. At the same time, the body of Mihir is also being stretchered out, surrounded by guests and family members. The hotel entrance doors swing open, and the sounds of the ambulance and police sirens whoosh in. It is an ocean of waiting journalists and TV crews outside. Undeterred, the ambulances part the paparazzi ocean and drive away into the darkness, and all is quiet again.

* * *

2

The hospital room is peaceful except for the intermittent beeping of monitors. Rajiv lies motionless on the adjustable bed, his head elevated, his face covered with an oxygen mask. His wrist has been bandaged, but a spot of blood has materialized on the gauze and is spreading. Inspector Apte stands close by, gazing intently at Rajiv but lost in thought. The doctor enters the room and inspects the data chart hanging on the side of Rajiv's bed.

'When can he talk, doctor?' asks Inspector Apte.

'Not for a few hours, at least,' says the doctor. 'He lost a lot of blood. The suicide attempt nearly made him go into a coma. Swallowing half a bottle of sleeping pills, and with that belt noose nearly cutting off oxygen supply to the brain; it's a miracle he's still alive.'

Apte nods. 'We'll be right here the second he is able to open his mouth.'

'Won't be till tomorrow, I promise you,' says the doctor.

Just at that moment, Rajiv goes into seizures, his body writhing uncontrollably, his flailing arms dislodging the connecting tubes. The doctor rushes to catch the falling drip stand. He shouts for the nurses. Inspector Apte steps back to let in other doctors who quickly form a ring around Rajiv. Their frantic calls are drowned by the multiple staccato beeps of various monitors.

Apte, not knowing how to react, draws the curtain a little and glances out of the window. The body of Mihir Kothari, post autopsy, is being transferred into a hearse, watched intently by a silent crowd. He turns away. The room has quietened now. Rajiv has been stabilized. Apte asks one of his colleagues to leave the room with him, while directing the other to keep a constant vigil.

* * *

The Kothari mansion bears a sombre look. The façade, which a few hours ago was festooned with a million flowers and twinkling LED curtains, is now an exposed cement behemoth—grey and melancholic as it catches the first light of day. Inside, in the colossal welcoming hall, Mihir's body has been kept for the *antim darshan*. The air-conditioned enclosure is bedecked with flowers, wreaths and garlands. Encircling the casket is a constant throng of mourners. They trace the wood and glass enclosure with their palms, which they take to their hearts, before stepping away and moving on. A few feet away sits the entire Kothari clan, dressed in white, their eyes shrouded by dark glasses. Beyond them, in neat rows that go all the way up to the entrance, are mourners, most of whom were guests at the birthday dinner the previous night. They sit on the floor cross-legged and stare into the distance, their demeanour amplifying the gloom that seems to have thickened the air inside. The police commissioner enters the hall and walks to the front to pay his respects, following which he joins the Kotharis, expressing his condolences. Rupesh takes him to the side. Neelima trails close behind.

'The autopsy report confirms death by cyanide poisoning,' the commissioner informs Rupesh.

Rupesh closes his eyes and embraces Neelima. 'I want him hung. You hear me, Commissioner?'

'Don't worry, sir. The case is watertight. He'll hang all right.'

'Where is he right now, the bastard?'

'Hinduja hospital. He hasn't regained consciousness yet. We are keeping a watch.'

'What did you mean when you said watertight?'

'Other than the scores of eyewitnesses, of course, we have him on CCTV, adding the cyanide to the soufflé. He's gone. Trust me, sir.'

Rupesh exhales but continues to stare at the commissioner, relenting only when the latter looks away, embarrassed. 'I don't want him gone; I want him dead. I want daily updates.'

'Yes, sir. If that's all . . .'

Rupesh shakes the commissioner's extended hand irritably—he knows the commissioner wants a public display of his close association with the Kotharis. But there are appearances that need to be maintained. He takes Neelima by her shoulder and walks away to once again sit cross-legged among the mourners, watching silently the shards of sunlight filter through the stained-glass windows and drench the casket.

* * *

The top-floor hallway, now bathed in sunlight, is eerily quiet, save for Inspector Apte's snoring and the occasional footsteps of the nurses and medical staff.

Apte's colleague, Constable Ganesh, fetches him tea and gently nudges his shoulder. The inspector shoots up from the sofa with a start and smothers his face with his hand in reflex.

Ganesh suppresses a smile and switches on the TV. Every channel is covering Mihir Kothari's funeral. The prime minister and the president have flown in from Delhi. The body has not yet arrived for the last rites—it is still at the Kothari mansion to afford the mourners a last glimpse—but huge crowds have built up already at the Colaba crematorium and taken over every available vantage spot, rooftops of adjacent and overlooking buildings included. The mood is solemn. People are still in shock. The financial gurus are dreading the opening of the Bombay Stock Exchange. The Kothari Group of Companies is all set to take a terrible beating. There is talk of suspending trading for a couple of days, until the Group announces its interim chairman, and the markets achieve some stability.

Ganesh continues to flick channels, landing at a Hindi news network that is recreating the tragic events of the previous night. *Khooni Bawarchi*, screams the running ticker, with a background score that would put a Ramsay brothers flick to shame. They are really going after Rajiv. Every little morsel of his past is being excavated, every tweet or social media post dredged up mercilessly, and with incandescent rage. The motives have been ascribed. He is being labelled an ISI agent. Meanwhile, the sentence has already been handed out—death by hanging. The Mumbai Bar Association is warning any lawyer from taking up Rajiv's defence. 'We will hang you before we hang Rajiv,' they howl. Apte snatches the remote from Ganesh's hand. He switches the TV off and tosses away the remote. He gets up and stretches his legs. His day has just begun. And it is going to be long and taxing— already he sees multiple missed calls from the higher-ups, from the commissioner to the minister's conduits. Just then, a nurse arrives with news of Rajiv regaining consciousness. 'Let's get to work,' Apte tells his colleagues, dusting his cap as he grabs it from the table.

Inspector Apte enters Rajiv's suite to find him awake and watchful. A little too watchful judging by his wide-eyed stare, which appears to be a drug-induced reaction. He twitches every now and then to adjust his head, propped awkwardly against the headrest by one of the nurses. The oxygen mask hangs by the IV stand now. The doctor asks Apte to restrict the questioning to no more than ten minutes.

'Has anyone spoken to him? Or told him what has transpired? Has he seen the news, read the papers?' enquires Apte.

The doctor shakes his head. 'He regained consciousness barely five minutes ago. You are the first one in. His vitals are stable. But he is still under heavy medication. Go easy on him.'

Apte strides over and pulls up a chair next to Rajiv's bed. They maintain eye contact for longer than both would have wished. 'Tell us everything. In your own words,' begins Inspector Apte.

'Inspector, I should be the one asking the questions,' says Rajiv, his speech heavy.

The tone annoys Inspector Apte. 'No. We ask, you answer,' he snaps.

'What is there to ask?' says Rajiv. 'I do not understand. Why am I in a hospital? How did I get here? What am I being treated for? Why is my wrist bandaged? Why is my voice croaky? Why does my head feel like it is being crushed under the wheels of a truck? Why is—'

'Let me add two more questions to your long list,' interjects Inspector Apte. 'Why did you murder Mihir Kothari? And why did you try to commit suicide?'

Rajiv is stunned. 'What are you talking about? What do you mean, "I murdered Mihir"? Is this some joke? Why, what has happened to Mihir? And suicide? I tried to commit suicide? Why would I do that? What is going on?'

Apte's colleagues, who are recording the interrogation on a camera, look at each other and sneer. They know Inspector Apte's patience runs thin.

'Mr Mehra, I am stating this only for the camera,' says Apte, grinding his teeth and trying not to appear angry. 'Yesterday night, we found you unconscious. You had swallowed half a bottle of sleeping pills. You had slashed your wrist. You had tried to strangle yourself using your own belt. You simultaneously tried three different methods to end your life—first time I have seen someone do this. And yet here you are, alive and breathing. Can't say the same for Mihir Kothari. He is dead. He is being cremated right now. You murdered him. That's that. Now. Tell me—'

Rajiv winces in pain. 'You must be crazy. Why would I commit suicide? Why would I kill Mihir? I loved and admired him. Why? How?'

Inspector Apte slams his *baint* in the hollow of his palm. 'I've had enough of this, *bhen chod*. There are witnesses to your actions last night. There are witnesses to your attempted suicide. You poisoned Mihir with cyanide. I have seen the autopsy report. You were his taster, no one else but you. He trusted you with his life. And now he is dead.'

Rajiv holds his face in his hands. 'Inspector Apte, this is all a terrible mix-up. I love the Kotharis. What could my motive possibly be? It's embarrassing to be even asking you this.'

'Don't worry. We'll get to the bottom of that soon,' says Apte. 'Meanwhile, you will be shifted to Arthur Road Jail hospital straightaway.'

'Mihir is dead . . . ' mumbles Rajiv. 'Why? Why would anyone want to—?'

'You tell me, Mehra sahab. You watched him die,' says Apte. 'You watched him. Hiding behind a curtain, you watched him die. And then you tried to slip out. You tell me why.'

'This is not possible,' says Rajiv. 'This cannot be happening. I was in the kitchen all the time. Ask anyone. Ask the chefs, ask the cooks, attendants, waiters, anyone.'

'What time?'

'Evening. Ask them. Why would I lie?'

'What time, I asked,' repeats Apte.

'I don't know. But the dinner had ended. We were readying the next course. The last course,' says Rajiv.

'What happened afterwards?' asks Apte.

'I was busy preparing the last course. Ask anyone, ask Emanuele Tardelli. He was the chef helping me. We were having an animated conversation on how to best position the glazing. The next thing I know is I'm talking with you just now. I am on a hospital bed. My wrist is bandaged. My head feels like it is about to explode. That's it; that is what I recollect.'

'You think this is funny, Mr Mehra?' says Apte. 'There are hundreds of witnesses who saw you trying to slip out from behind the curtain after watching Mihir Kothari die a gruesome death. Hundreds more saw you in the lobby as we were taking you to the police station. Dozens heard you request us to allow you to collect your medicines and insulin. Dozens more saw you take the lift with us to your suite. On the fourth floor, the housekeeping staff saw you enter your room along with us. Inside the room, the three of us saw you go to the toilet.'

Inspector Apte inches closer to Rajiv and growls. 'We forced the toilet door open. We found you unconscious. You had slit your wrist. There was blood everywhere. And this—' Apte snatches at Rajiv's gown,'—this bruise on your neck? This is from your own belt.'

Rajiv recoils in horror.

Apte rubs his wrist in the hollow of the palm of his other hand by way of habit. *'Bhen chod, mazaak hai kya? Chutiya samajh rakhaa hai humay?* You are claiming all this is a lie?'

Before Rajiv can react, the door bursts open and a man rushes in. 'Rajiv, don't say a word.'

Inspector Apte is at the end of his tether. 'And who the hell are you?' he shouts. A moment later he recognizes the man. Ajay Bansal, the famous criminal lawyer.

'Never mind who I am. Who the fuck are you?' fires back Ajay.

Inspector Apte knows the drill. He swallows his anger and responds, this time calmly. 'Inspector Apte.'

'Well, whoever you are, and whoever these two are,' scoffs Ajay, glancing at Ganesh and Tukaram, 'consider yourself suspended by tomorrow.'

Ganesh and Tukaram switch the camera off instinctively and begin dismantling and gathering up the tripod.

'Rajiv,' says Ajay, 'Have these guys been interviewing you? What have you told them?'

Rajiv doesn't respond; shock is writ large on his face.

Inspector Apte collects his wits. 'Mr Bansal, we are taking him to Arthur Road.'

'On whose authority?' demands Ajay. 'And did you interview my client? Were you recording it?'

Inspector Apte looks away. 'We weren't interviewing him, sir. We saved his life. We just came to enquire how he was doing.'

'Enough with your concern,' snaps Ajay. 'I want a copy of the recording. Let me be the judge of whether you were enquiring about his health or conducting an interview. You can leave now.'

Inspector Apte knows when he is beaten; every policeman does. He tries to salvage some pride through terseness. 'We will be back with a warrant. It is an open and shut case. We'll be filing a chargesheet by this evening.'

'Or so you think,' says Ajay. 'I will be filing a chargesheet against the three of you if you don't leave the room on a count of five. One. Two. Three . . .'

Once outside, having gently closed the door behind him and heard it click, Apte punches the wall, hard, and treads down the corridor, fuming. Ganesh and Tukaram decide to follow a safe distance behind.

'*Aukaat dikha di Bansal ne, bhen chod*,' cries Apte. '*Sun rahe ho*, Ganesh? *Ek mahine ke ander latkaya nahin is gandu ko toh mera naam Apte nahin*,' he adds, without turning his head to look back. He is addressing the air in front of him. Ganesh and Tukaram understand, of course. 'Yes, sir. It's an open and shut case,' they say in unison.

* * *

The Colaba crematorium is teeming with mourners. The unprecedented outpouring of love and affection can only be attributed to the fact that they, along with millions of other Indians, saw Mihir as the true inheritor and keeper of Mohanbhai Kothari's legacy. And now they bid farewell to the man who made them wealthy beyond their dreams. The road outside is lined with them till the eye can see. They shower rose petals at the convoy as it passes by and enters the crematorium gates. The casket is lowered from the open truck and carried inside by members of the Kothari family. The cremation platform is surrounded by rows of Bollywood stars, politicians and business tycoons. As the body is placed on it and the pyre lit, thick smoke envelops the gathering. It swells and rises skyward against the backdrop of the setting sun.

Watching the funeral unfold live on TV is Rajiv Mehra in his hospital room. As the camera zooms in on Subhadra Kothari crying inconsolably, tears flow down Rajiv's cheeks. He still cannot believe it. He looks away, lost in thought. A moment later he reaches for his phone and plays an old clip. It is of Subhadra's wedding celebration.

The dinner was on a moonlit night at a beach in Phuket. Rajiv swipes to increase the volume. Everyone is laughing and enjoying themselves. Giant marquees have been set up on the beach, close to the water, their poles festooned with flowers. Live music plays in the vicinity. The sound distracts the person shooting the clip and she swings the phone in its direction.

The band members smile and wave a polite acknowledgement. A waiter carrying a tray of wine glasses abruptly enters the frame and trips, spilling red wine on Rajiv. The person shooting the video breaks into a hearty laugh. The camera sways from the waiter to Mihir in the background to Rajiv again, brushing his wine-soaked linen jacket with a handkerchief. 'Look up, Rajiv!' begs the woman shooting the video. Rajiv looks up bashfully and then steps out of the frame with an awkward smile. The camera, as though hunting for another subject, enters one of the tents. Guests are seated at round tables and there is much laughter and merriment as waiters rush in and out, serving the many courses. The waters slip inside the tent from time to time, skimming over the guests' bare feet, extracting oohs and aahs when they recede. Subhadra and Rohit cut the wedding cake as a beaming Mihir looks on. Rajiv pauses the clip and zooms in on the laughing Subhadra.

He looks up at the TV and at the visuals of her crying. It is too much to take. He weeps uncontrollably, trying to stifle his sobs with his fist.

Outside the room, the policemen notice but decide not to pay heed. They have a much more important job at hand. Briskly, they stand to attention. The door is pushed open and Inspector Apte strides in. Alongside him is a forlorn looking Ajay Bansal. Apte slaps down the warrant and the police custody order on Rajiv's bed. He stares hard at Rajiv, then at the TV and then at the lawyer. 'Tukaram!' he shouts. 'Confiscate the phone of the accused. Dump his belongings in a bag. He is coming with us to Arthur Jail. Right now.'

* * *

The employees and staff of the Kothari Group have lined the corridors of each of the nineteen floors of the office complex. A thousand men and women standing shoulder to shoulder, silently, not one murmur, not one sound. They are waiting for Rupesh and other members of the Kothari family to arrive at the headquarters. The wait has lasted more than an hour already. Meanwhile, barely a mile away, the Kothari family waits, too, on six folding chairs. Rupesh, Neelima, Vrinda, Rohan, Subhadra, Miraben and Viramani look into the distance, at the pyre that still smoulders, although most of it has turned into a scarred battlefield of ash. Half a dozen priests rummage through the mound, chanting shlokas. They scoop up the ashes and pour them into a shallow mortar pan one of them cradles in his arms. Birds chirp all around as the first rays of the sun pierce through the green canopy and fall on the smouldering remnants of the pyre.

Approaching the Kotharis, the head priest places the mortar pan on a bench a few feet in front of them and walks away. Vrinda is the first to rise from her chair; the others let her reach the bench and then get up from their respective seats and follow. Vrinda sees the heap of ash and in it, eight rings. She breaks down and is about to collapse to the ground when Neelima catches her and props her up, patting her head and stroking her hair. Rupesh walks up and embraces both. His eyes have welled up, but gazing at the rings peeping through the ash, they reflect something other than sadness and loss. It is anger that has taken hold of Rupesh. He asks the priest to transfer the contents of the mortar pan into an urn.

* * *

As Rupesh proceeds through the office corridors with the urn, the employees step forward one by one and touch the urn and then their foreheads. The procession builds floor by floor, quietly, determinedly, and by the time it reaches the top floor, where Mihir used to sit, and where Rupesh sits now, it has transformed into a giant throbbing mass of humanity. Rupesh enters the office and places the urn in front of Mihir's portrait. He bows reverentially and retreats. Vrinda comes forward, accompanied by Neelima, and lights an incense stick.

Once the crowd has dispersed, the Kothari family gathers in Mihir's office, in silence, staring at the urn, the portrait, the burning joss stick and the eight rings that have been arranged in a circle around the urn. Prodded by Rupesh, the Kotharis move to the anteroom where some food has been arranged. None of them is hungry; no one touches the food—sandwiches, salad and pastries. It lies on the giant mahogany table, resplendent yet lifeless.

* * *

The polpette di melanzane is out of this world. Boiled eggplants, soaked bread, basil, garlic and lots of pecorino. Deep-fried. He stops chewing and lets the taste linger, allowing the crust to melt slowly. Then, reluctantly, he swallows it down. The eyes stay firmly shut.

Next arrives the main course—octopus and calamari, fried eggplant, granita of lemon, orange and ginger, accompanied by Feudo Disisa Grillo, white; and to finish, cannoli.

He takes his time. Easy, because the concept of it no longer exists. The background murmur of indistinct conversations only adds to the magical evening. The lighting is dim and the music soothing.

Then comes the slap.

Rajiv peels away from the damp wall with a start. The cell echoes with the laughter of his fellow inmates.

'Eat!' orders the guard, pushing the thali towards Rajiv with his boot. It has one burnt chapatti and a bowl of thin yellow liquid.

But I have just finished my dinner, Rajiv almost blurts. He nods instead and slumps once more against the wall. The metal door bangs shut, and the cell returns to its sounds—burps and farts and snores and the trickle of pee.

As with time, there is no concept of privacy. It is strangely liberating but only after one gets used to it.

Rajiv hasn't touched prison supper for a week running. Memory is feeding him. Recollections are his source of calories. He has been meticulous, as is his habit. The first night, while his fellow inmates forced the burnt chapatti and foul dal down their throats, Rajiv had feasted on crunchy pork shoulder with tangy mostarda fruits and a truly exquisite smoked potato purée. All he had to do was prop his back against the wall, hug his bended knees and close his eyes. The music came and brought with it dishes he had prepared weeks, months, even years ago. *The personification of memory*. What madeleines were to Proust, tortellini Genovese is to Rajiv. Day one: cut of Chianina steak with a Barolo reduction and guinea fowl torchons; day two: foie gras on brioche with poached apples, raspberry sauce and a little ball of foie gras pâté crusted with pistachios; day three: 1998 Amarone de valpolicella, tarte Tatin with vanilla creme fraiche and rabbit polpette served on a richly flavoured carrot purée; day four: Fior di Latte, blanched and grilled vegetables, rice salad, pork meatballs, a stunning recipe of pork tripe with potatoes, and poached veal; day five: anchovy 'ice cream' with sardines, pine nuts, raisins and a steak done rare with a Marsala and anchovy demiglace . . .

Today is day six; and even though Rajiv has finished his dinner and licked his lips in satisfaction, he is worried. His memory has begun to fail him. Perhaps it is to do with the arduous act of playing chess with himself in his mind every day, for hours on end—all those squares and letters and numbers, their constant jangling and fighting inside his brain. Memory has been granted a way to make up the hours when it isn't pulled up for the purpose of putting food on the table. There's only so much one can recollect with precision. And now, to his horror, he can't recollect his dinner for tomorrow. This is a catastrophe. 'Think,' he says to himself, slapping his head with his fist. 'Think, Rajiv,' he cries, 'or you will sleep hungry tomorrow.'

'Do you want to eat this?'

A burly man is leaning over Rajiv. He recoils instinctively.

'Well? Shall I?' asks the man, pointing to the thali.

Rajiv nods. The man snatches the chapatti from the thali and stuffs it in his mouth, as though worried Rajiv might go back on his word. Next, he picks up the bowl with both hands and raises it to his mouth, emptying it in one swift movement.

Wiping his mouth, he trudges to the far end of the cell where the other five inmates are busy in a game of cards. They make space for him to sit.

The lights go out. A candle is lit amid furious curses.

Assorted arancini and panzerotti with pink gin and tonic, sighs Rajiv and closes his eyes. 'No,' he says to himself, 'that's not good enough for tomorrow. Think!'

The demands made by a human body are few. It can be trained. Mind over matter. Thoughts can be stacked. Associations discarded. Friendships forgotten. Breathing and ablutions—that's all there is to life. And prison is where one can carve out this minimalism of human architecture.

Eyes. Visual pleasure is the first to go, followed soon by pleasures received through the rest of the senses: sound, smell, taste, touch. How easy it is to turn functioning organs into vestigial. All one needs is a prison cell. Directed evolution, is what it is. Put a man in a cage and he returns to his roots. The speed with which this training proceeds can be frightening. The first day is the most difficult, of that there is never any doubt. From then on, it is up to you. There can be no pain if there is no association. I am clothed but I can train myself to be naked. I can be happy if I lose hope. As hope recedes, calm descends. Life begins anew.

Rajiv smiles, thinking of friends and fights and recipes and deadlines and the endless loop of daily existence. Oh, the fickleness of it all. How easy it is to scrunch them all up like yesterday's newspaper and toss them over your shoulder. How easy. But isn't hope linked to memory? Recollection is a poor substitute for physical presence but it still is one. Is my memory not my friend right now? It is feeding me, supporting me, helping me bide time. How do I discard it; wipe the slate clean? Spaghetti alla Siracusana with pine nuts, sardines, raisins, breadcrumbs, capers, and to finish, a ricotta and pistachio cake. *Damn, this whole situation is impossible. Think, Rajiv. Think!*

* * *

It is a typical grey, wet day in London as a young man in a quilted jacket and a cap enters Magdeleine Tussauds. He checks his wristwatch, a Rolex Submariner with a navy-blue dial. Inside, the hall is bustling with visitors and tourists, their excited voices echoing in the vastness.

He slows as he passes by the section that has wax figures of Indian actors, politicians and celebrities. The one of Rajiv Mehra, in his trademark chef's attire with a rolling pin in hand, is unusually popular; sightseers cluster around, clicking selfies with the grinning Rajiv.

The man shoves through the crowd and enters a long corridor leading to the museum basement. Once there, he grabs a janitor's trolley parked on the side and tows it along a row of offices, drawing out an ID card from his jeans and clipping it to his jacket as he trundles along, playing the part. Arriving at a double door, he brings the trolley to a halt, pushes the cap further down on his head and peers through a glass-panelled door.

The dimly lit room is a storage area-cum-workshop, crammed with busts and wax replicas. At the far end sits an old man touching up a wax head with his brush, applying his strokes with care, his eye secured on a magnifying table lens. Classical opera is playing on the radio nearby. He swivels the lens away and straightens up, admiring his work with a few tilts of his head. 'That should do. Nice work, Mr Appleby,' he mumbles approvingly to himself, picking up his coffee mug as he does so.

Outside, in the corridor, the man in the quilted jacket moves away from the pane and strolls on, abandoning the trolley as he exits through to the stairway.

It is drizzling as Mr Appleby emerges from the rear entrance of Magdeleine Tussauds. He stops at a kiosk to buy a sandwich and a pack of cigarettes. Across the road, the man in the quilted jacket is watching him. He flicks his cigarette away and crosses the road, maintaining a safe distance. Mr Appleby is in no hurry, walking at a leisurely pace as he munches on his sandwich.

Arriving at a bus stop, he parks himself inside, pulling out a book from his leather bag. Watching his every move, the man in the quilted jacket has taken shelter under a shop awning ten yards away. A few moments later, a double-decker rolls in, and Mr Appleby climbs aboard, taking a seat by the nearest window. Just as the bus is about to exit the bay, the man tailing him hops on, climbing up to the deck above.

There is heavy traffic. Fifteen minutes pass by. The double-decker finally leaves downtown and enters the suburbs. The man in the quilted jacket is getting restless. He has had to screen every passenger getting off at the many halts, as Appleby is not in his direct sight. Eventually, the bus reaches the old man's stop. The man in the quilted jacket spots him and gets down as well. They walk a fair distance. It has started to drizzle again. The man in the quilted jacket curses and turns up his collar.

Mr Appleby's house is a semi-detached property in a desolate street. A cat exits as he pushes open the main door. He dumps his leather bag on the sofa, hangs his overcoat on the stand outside the living room, and proceeds upstairs to run his bath.

The man in the quilted jacket walks up stealthily to the house and then the entrance. He unlocks the main door softly. As he enters, the cat scampers in. The sounds of classical opera fill the air inside. The man climbs the stairs unhurriedly, with the music getting louder as he reaches the first floor.

He enters the bedroom. It is crammed with busts and masks and templates. He can hear the sloshing of the water in the bathtub. He steps forward quietly and peeks inside the bathroom through the door that is ajar.

Mr Appleby is lying supine in the bathtub, his eyes closed. A scented candle burns on the rim, alongside an ashtray that contains a lit cigarette. A glass of wine is on the floor by the tub. The man in the quilted jacket waits for the opportune moment. The music intensifies.

He rushes forward and pounces on the old man. Mr Appleby is in no position to react. He thrashes his arms and bobs his head and tries to scream, but it is futile. A second later, his limp body slides down to the bottom of the bathtub. Silence descends.

The man in the quilted jacket spills the wine around the bathtub. He picks up the cigarette and drops it on the upturned book. He uses the candle to set fire to the curtain. As the curtain catches fire, the man slips out of the bathroom. Outside in the bedroom he is confronted by the blank stare of the cat that has settled on the bed pillow. Unconcerned, he strides over to the wardrobe and sweeps the contents to the floor. He is looking for something.

He finds it eventually. Three thick wads of hundred-pound currency notes. Slipping them in the inside pocket of his jacket, he runs down the stairs and out of the house, walking away at a brisk pace. The neighbours have already spotted thick smoke billowing out of Mr Appleby's bathroom window. He quickens his pace and disappears down the turn in the road. Two hundred yards down, he takes shelter at a bus stop. As he waits, fire engines rush past, sirens wailing.

He checks his Rolex for the time and hails a cab.

3

The lights come on with a heavy clunk of the lever. A baton drags over the cells' metal doors. Whistles echo in the halls. Boots stomp in the gangways. The pooled effect of these sounds is terrifying.

Rajiv wakes up with a shudder. His fellow inmates are up already. They have arranged themselves in a line. Rajiv climbs down from his bunk and joins the end of the line. A key jangles in the lock and the door opens. The guard orders the inmates to assemble outside their cell. Within a few minutes, the corridors are crammed with men rubbing their eyes and scratching their balls. It is 5 a.m.

'Attention!' barks the wing officer and initiates the march. The inmates, collected in groups, await their turn and join this procession as it snakes through the gangways and halls and comes to a halt at the toilets. The entire ritual is accomplished with clockwork precision. Each prisoner is provided with a towel and a quarter portion of soap and a *datun*. Rajiv takes his due, putting the datun in his mouth and walking on. Arriving at the communal sink—an open cube of crudely assembled granite with a generous veneer of algae and spirogyra swaying as though to music—he spits the bitter froth out and proceeds to the shower cubicles. The cubicles are doorless and without showerheads. A rusted pipe runs through each, piercing the separating walls like an arrow let go. The pipe buds out a plastic tap inside each booth. The tap cannot be turned off or on. Presently, water gushes from it with great speed and sound, filling up cracked and handle-less plastic buckets, making the plastic mugs inside them bob up and down. This is the story of every cubicle. Each inmate has exactly three minutes to take a bath, after which he is evicted and the next one takes his spot. But the taps keep running. When the taps stop, bathing stops, no matter if the inmate is all lathered up.

Rajiv goes down on his haunches and scoops up a mug of freezing cold water. He pours it over his head. His body shudders, his teeth chatter, his lips quiver, but he repeats the process. He is applying soap, his eyes firmly shut, when a man slithers in at lightning speed and stabs his shoulder with a screwdriver.

Rajiv tumbles over, recoiling in pain. The screwdriver is jutting out of his shoulder, but he cannot see it. His head comes under the running tap as the bucket skids away. His assaulter, a scrawny man of not more than twenty, has grabbed Rajiv from behind—a pincer hold—and is not letting go. Blood is spraying out of Rajiv's shoulder. Rajiv manages to pry open his eyes. He pushes his arms out to loosen his assaulter's grip. He tries to get up but slips. Sensing his moment the assaulter relaxes his grip, only to pluck out the screwdriver with his free hand. He tries to stab Rajiv again but misses the shoulder.

Rajiv is helpless, bleeding profusely, writhing on the floor, and with his face still lathered up, he can't see much beyond a foot. The screwdriver descends. And this time it is the thigh. Rajiv screams with all his might. He is about to lose consciousness. But just as the attacker is about to stab Rajiv right in the eye, a guard enters the cubicle and grabs him by his neck and wrenches him off Rajiv. The guard is strong and well built. He lifts the attacker clean off the ground and flings him against the wall. The sound of bones being crushed brings Rajiv some respite and the hope that he is safe. But the attacker is undeterred. He picks his mangled body up and charges at Rajiv one more time. 'I'll kill you, you bastard,' he screams; 'I'll kill you—you destroyed my family.'

Unfortunately for him, the guard is ready and waiting. He slaps the assaulter hard. '*Tu* Kothari *hai ke, bhen chod?*' he asks, prompting a ripple of laughter among the crowd that has collected. Meanwhile, the commotion has brought in more guards. They whisk the assaulter away, probably to throw him in solitary for a week or two. For Rajiv, it is the clinic. The doctor stitches him up and tells the officer that Rajiv needs an overnight stay at the prison infirmary, as the risk of infection if he returns to his cell is real. The officer nods reluctantly. A guard strides over to shackle Rajiv's hand to the bed. Rajiv is exhausted and in pain, but he ekes out a thin smile. 'Where will I run off to?' he confronts the guard.

'It is to protect you,' comes the unsure reply.

The officer approaches Rajiv. 'Do you know why that man tried to kill you?' he asks.

'I have no idea.'

'He is an unemployed graduate, or *sikshit berozgar* as we call them. In the clanger for petty theft. Comes from a lower middle-class family. Father retired as a TTE, mother gives music tuitions, sister does odd tailoring jobs. They put together all their savings to buy a few Kothari shares, in the hope that they'd be able to manage their daughter's wedding with the returns. Then you entered the frame. And killed Mihir Kothari. The stocks plummeted. The family lost everything. The news reached the son. All he had was the screwdriver.'

* * *

'Tell him the truth; don't hide anything,' whispers Police Commissioner Satyaprakash Singh.

'Yes, sir,' replies Apte.

'In my experience, telling the truth embarrasses them, makes them uncomfortable. And later on, when they ask you to hide it, and you do, they owe you one, if you know what I mean,' adds the commissioner.

'I do, sir,' smiles Apte. The two men are waiting in the lobby of the Kothari Company headquarters at Colaba. Apte distracts himself and looks out the giant window that makes up one entire wall of the lobby. The view is spectacular. They are on the nineteenth floor; Mumbai appears liveable from the skies.

The secretary comes over to let them know that Rupesh Kothari will be with them in five minutes. Commissioner Singh turns to Apte again. 'You tell him the facts. He will decide what is to be done next. Clear?'

The heavy wooden doors release, and the policemen are let in. Rupesh Kothari gets up from his chair and walks over to shake hands with the commissioner, who introduces him to Inspector Apte. 'Inspector Apte here has been handling our investigation. There are a few things we'd like to discuss with you, sir.'

'Please have a seat,' says Rupesh. It has been a week since he took over as the chairman of the Kothari Group. The turbulence resulting from Mihir's murder, both in the market as well as within the Group, has lessened considerably. The company's stock has stabilized. Things are getting back to normal, or as normal as they can be, given the circumstances. Mihir's death continues to remain in the headlines, but some astute media management has meant that Rupesh, condemned for years by the same media as Mihir's playboy bachelor brother, has now been reborn as a thoughtful businessman, more than capable of managing the Kothari Group.

A giant portrait of Mihir hangs next to Mohanbhai Kothari. The policemen gape at it reverentially.

'Shall we begin?' asks Rupesh.

Inspector Apte waits for a nod from his boss. 'Go on, Apte,' says the commissioner.

'The investigation is complete, sir,' says Apte. 'The case is watertight. We have eyewitnesses; we have the CCTV footage; we have the medical opinions. There is no doubt whatsoever that Rajiv Mehra will hang to death for his crime. The only question remaining is of his motive.'

Rupesh fidgets in his seat. 'And what is your conclusion? What was his motive?'

The commissioner steps in. 'That is why we are having this meeting. We would like you to decide. We will put before you all possibilities.'

Rupesh expresses surprise. 'Wait a minute. You say the case is watertight and yet you aren't sure of the motive? Then what is the—'

'Let me put it this way, sir,' interjects the commissioner, 'It would be better, for the family and the Kothari Group, if you were to decide which line we should take. There are three possible motives we have narrowed in on—that Rajiv Mehra was having a stormy affair with a member of the Kothari family, that the promise by the Kotharis to help him open a chain of international restaurants fell through and finally, that he was working at the behest of China Telecom.'

Rupesh is stunned.

'Of the Chinese possibility, we have no proof,' says the commissioner. 'But we can manufacture it, if you think that is the line we should take.'

Rupesh shakes his head. 'No, you shouldn't. Bringing in China will seriously dent our investments in that country—and they aren't limited to telecom, mind you. The worst hit would be our oil exploration and mining ventures. Tell me more about the other two possibilities.'

'Well, I'll be honest with you, Mr Kothari. They are at best conjecture.'

'Conjecture?'

'Yes, but based on facts.'

'A conjecture based on facts. Well, go on then. I am all eyes and ears.'

The commissioner prods Apte to take over. He untangles the laces of a file cover and commences placing call detail records on the table. The commissioner restrains himself for a good minute before he's had enough. He extends his arm to prevent Apte from arranging the documents any further. 'Not necessary, Apte. Just mention the summary to Mr Kothari.'

'Right, sir,' replies Apte awkwardly. 'Of all the calls Rajiv Mehra made to the Kothari family over the last three years, 15 per cent were to Mr Mihir Kothari, 5 per cent were to Rohit Kothari, 2 per cent were to you, and the rest . . .'

'Go on,' urges Rupesh.

'And the rest, 78 per cent, to Mrs Neelima Kothari Thapar. Your sister.'

Rupesh glares at Apte and then at the commissioner. 'What nonsense. Where are you going with this?'

The commissioner intervenes hurriedly. 'Nowhere, Mr Kothari. These are just the facts. It is up to you. The China angle has already been rejected. We cannot secure a conviction without claiming a strong motive. I hope you understand that.'

'Yes, but I don't want the family name to be splashed all over the news like this—an affair with a cook. Neelima is my dear sister. There might have been other reasons for his calling her up so much.'

'Like what,' smirks Apte then checks himself and lowers his head.

Rupesh scowls at the commissioner. 'The affair claim is out of the question. The Kothari Group is barely out of the woods yet. We can't afford a scandal. And I won't allow my sister's name to be sullied like this.'

The commissioner nods. 'That leaves us with the final possibility. Rajiv was incensed that his restaurant chain proposal fell through.'

'Yes. Go with that,' says Rupesh.

'We would need to arrange for documents in this regard. Emails, paper trail, etc.'

'That shouldn't be a problem. Viramani here will help you,' says Rupesh, turning to his right-hand man.

'We'd need the documentation by tomorrow, sir,' says the commissioner.

'You will have it by tonight,' assures Viramani.

'If we are done here, commissioner, I have a meeting right now I cannot get out of,' says Rupesh.

'Sure, sir,' replies the commissioner, he and Apte getting up.

Rupesh shakes their hands warmly. 'I cannot thank you enough.'

'Please don't mention it, sir. It is the least we can do,' says the commissioner. Viramani leads him and Inspector Apte out of the room.

In the elevator, the commissioner exchanges a knowing glance with Apte. 'Watch and learn, Apte. Watch and learn,' he smiles.

'Always, sir,' says Apte. 'But sir, if I can ask you one question.'

'Shoot.'

'What according to you was Rajiv Mehra's motive?'

The elevator door slides open. The commissioner strides out, with Apte close behind, trying to catch up. 'Who cares, Apte. The judge will believe what he sees, but what he sees will be put in front of him by us, who see what we believe,' says the commissioner looking straight ahead.

'. . . and we see what Rupesh believes,' grins Apte.

The commissioner checks his step and turns to glare at Apte. There is a moment's delay that makes Apte distinctly uncomfortable, followed by a hearty laugh by the commissioner.

* * *

The sun is not yet up. The lush green meadows of the Italian Alps are dotted with a few grazing cows, their collar bells jingling lazily.

He is on the outskirts of the town of Cortina d'Ampezzo. The trail winds through a forest, and he can smell and taste the early morning dew. He quickens his pace, to reach a clearing sealed at one end by woodland. The only sound is of a gentle stream running over shingles, on its way to the Boite river.

He can see Emanuele Tardelli. There he is, ankle-deep in the gurgling water, wearing an anorak and a fisherman's floppy hat, his legs a little apart and his back arched back as he waits for the fish to take the bait.

He knew Emanuele would be here early in the morning; he likes to catch the fish that he serves in his restaurant. He creeps up behind Emanuele, grabbing a rock from the riverbed, timing his steps with the whipping sound the tackle makes every time Emanuele swings it over his head.

He clobbers Emanuele with the rock. It is a clean hit to the side of the skull. The impact is as sudden as it is fatal. Emanuele lets go of the fishing tackle and collapses in the water.

Waiting a good minute to make sure Emanuele is dead, he arranges the body on the shallow riverbed to make it appear as if Emanuele suffered a heart attack and drowned. He places Emanuele's head face down in the water and adjusts the dead man's fingers so they grip the fishing tackle. He flings Emanuele's floppy hat a fair distance downstream. Then he checks his Rolex. He might just be able to catch the morning bus back to Bolzano if he is lucky.

* * *

The police van drives through the Arthur Road Jail gates and comes to a halt in the open yard a little distance beyond.

Rajiv steps out and is escorted inside the prison. He is ordered to undress. He complies. He is screened and body-checked, thoroughly and intrusively, after which he is asked to put on the change provided. His possessions, a wristwatch and a pen, are registered and taken away. He is marched along with other prisoners to the main compound.

Rajiv knows the routine by now. Today is the fifth day of his court appearance. Life is hell. But this is just the beginning. His lawyer Ajay Bansal has tried every possible trick in the book but to little avail. No politician or judge is willing to help. When you are accused of murdering Mihir Kothari, even God would think twice before extending a helping hand. The case has been transferred to a fast-track court. The judge has given an assurance that the verdict will be delivered within a month. The hearings are being conducted daily. Today, the prosecution presented evidence before the court, and as Inspector Apte explained the details to the judge, Rajiv sat inside the dock, expressionless, knowing there was nothing that Bansal and his team could muster in defence. It doesn't come more open and shut than this. Inspector Apte has been exceptional in avoiding tumbling into the usual loopholes and traps the defence lays out—a break in the chain of evidence, witnesses turning hostile, CCTV footage without the date and time stamp—there is nothing, nothing at all that Bansal has been able to find fault with. If anything, Rajiv is a little relieved at the pace of the trial; it might conclude sooner than the judge promised, a month. He knows what the sentence is going to be.

'Lights out!' screams the guard. One of Rajiv's cellmates gets up from his bunk bed and switches off the light. Rajiv continues to share the cell with six other prisoners. It is the governor's way of dealing with a suicide-watch case—let fellow prisoners watch and prevent the suicide.

The cell stinks. The Indian toilet in the corner has not been cleaned for two days and is overflowing. There is no ceiling fan, for obvious reasons. The ventilator is jammed shut. It is hot and humid. The prisoners are bare-chested. The stench of the sweat mixes with that of shit and sits heavy in the air. Rajiv has the upper bunk, only a few feet below the ceiling. He cannot sit on his bed. The claustrophobia is overpowering.

A joint is being passed around. It is offered to Rajiv, and he takes it. Anything that helps transport him from his present state of mind and body. The near total darkness in the cell aids in diffusing tension among the prisoners. There is no eye contact to be intimidated by. This is the best time in the whole day.

Rajiv takes a long drag at the joint and passes it on. The man who receives it holds it for a moment, as though for show, and says, '*Khabar suni aaj mainey. Tut toh latkeyga bhai. Pakka.*' Hearing this crisp sentence, almost out of nowhere, makes the rest of the inmates break into spontaneous laughter. '*Latkeyga, pakka,*' they repeat. Rajiv stares into the darkness for an extended moment and then joins in the merriment. It's a release. He cannot see the other prisoners, only hear their laughter, and this is comforting. '*Latkunga. Pakka,*' he says to the darkness, almost giggling. When the laughter ebbs, a prisoner asks him, 'Lawyer *nahin hai tere paas koi achcha?*'

'*Hai na,*' says Rajiv. 'Mumbai *ka* most expensive.'

The darkness laughs back, '*Loot raha hai tujhe wo, bhai.*'

Rajiv smiles and extends his hand for the joint.

A voice asks, 'We noticed no one has visited you here. You have no family? Besides us, of course.' More laughs.

'I don't,' says Rajiv. 'Well, not close enough for them to
come and visit me here.'

'No father? No mother?'

'Not anymore.'

'What happened to them?'

'They died when I was ten.'

'Cyanide poisoning?'

Rajiv is hurt at the vicious barb, but then gives in. The
darkness is not interested in showering him with compliments.
It is a mirror; uninhibited and unapologetic. He is opening his
heart to people who don't give a fuck. It is what he has wanted
all his life. He joins in the chuckles. 'No,' he says with a smirk
no one else can see, 'I could not procure it in time.'

'Tell us your story,' the darkness implores, at first a lone
voice but soon joined by a chorus. 'Yes, we want to know the
story of the great Rajiv Mehra. Maybe after you are dead, one
of us will write it as a book and become a millionaire.'

A voice shoots back at the suggestion, '*Bhosdike*, you can't
write your own name and you will write a book?'

Another voice slips in amid the raucous laughter. '*Chutiye
ne* tattoo *mein bhi apna naam* misspell *kiya hai*!'

Rajiv laughs heartily. 'What do you want to know?' he asks
of the darkness.

'Everything. Start with your parents. What happened to
them?'

Rajiv takes a long, unhurried drag. He waits, exhales,
passes the joint and begins. '*Char dham*. It all started with the
char dham.'

The darkness has heard Rajiv. It stays quiet and waits. No
quips or taunts. No banter. Just silence and anticipation.

Rajiv continues. '7 October 1991. We—my parents, grandparents, my sister, younger brother and I—we were on the *char dham* yatra. We were stationed at Gaurikund and about to commence our trek to Badrinath when we came under the force of a landslide. It was all so sudden; I still get the jitters thinking about that moment. I was ten. My parents, sister, younger brother, they were swept away right before my eyes. I held on to the protruding root of a tree. That's how I got saved. Their bodies were unearthed a week later. Just like that, in the snap of a finger, I lost everything. We were a joint family—my father and his elder brother, my tauji, had married my mother and her elder sister, my masi. Our ancestral house was in a small nook in Chandni Chowk, called Mumtaz Sarai. I was taken under the care of my tauji. Their's was a dysfunctional family—tauji was drunk most times and my masi, her calling was to pound the mortar with pestle and scheme all day long.

'The next few months were like the unfolding of a horror story. I was beaten regularly by my tauji, forced to run errands for him even during the day. I was thrown out of school because of it. Whenever I could, I would run away from my miserable existence and go and sit in front of the Sis Ganj Sahib gurdwara kitchen and just watch the proceedings. It was so calming, a world away from my drudgery. I would sit there for hours on end and watch people cook and eat. Years later I realized that watching someone eat is the most joyous of acts, probably more joyous than the act of eating itself. Sometimes I would dare to venture in and help out during a busy langar. The cooks were kind. They soon got to know me, to expect my presence, miss it even, when for some reason I couldn't show up.

'Soon, it became my family away from my family. I started to spend more and more of my time there. Within six months I was inducted formally into the gurdwara kitchen. They even paid me a small stipend. The food was, of course, free. And that is where I learnt to cook. The head cook, Wahe Guru Pal Singh ji, became like a grandfather to me. He loved to teach me how to cook. He loved to experiment. A refugee from Peshawar, and a fifth-generation cook, he knew so many recipes, it was incredible. The langar is always vegetarian, but he would teach me non-vegetarian dishes, especially on weekends. They say Moti Mahal, the famous restaurant in Daryaganj that claims to have invented butter chicken, used to employ Wahe Guru ji's brother, and that legendary recipe was actually his. Anyhow, years passed by. I turned sixteen. I was happy with my life, although I had not more than a thousand rupees as my life's savings. One day, an NRI Sikh family visited the gurudwara—a man named Gurpreet Singh, his wife and their two children. They stayed for the evening langar. As it happened, our head cook was on leave that day, and I stepped in. The NRI family loved the food. Gurpreet Singh ji ran a chain of hotels in Canada. Originally from Patiala, he had made millions in the logging business in Canada. He had a chat with Wahe Guru Singh ji the next day, and before I knew what was happening, I was on a flight to Ottawa. I landed in Canada with just a little suitcase and one change of clothes.

'When I finally left Canada, ten years later, it was on a private jet that belonged to David Beckham. To Dubai. God's been kind. Or should I say both Wahe Gurus have been kind.

'I won't bore you with my years in Canada. But you can guess. Ten glorious years, two Michelin stars, three restaurants,

nine dishes named after me, the keys to Ottawa and a gong by
the Canadian government—and I was all of twenty-six. The
next four years I spent in Dubai—conducting the chef armies
of the most luxurious hotels you can think of. And the last ten
have been spent at no fixed place—a citizen of the world, you
can say. And it all ends here. In a month.'

'Probably sooner,' quips the darkness.

'Yes. Probably sooner. I am ready for it.'

'No one is ready for it, bhai. No one. You think you are.
But when they slip the noose over your head and tighten it . . .'

'Anyway, that's my story.'

There is a pause, followed by the tiniest of applauses, just
to not offend the speaker. Then, a voice asks what has been
in the mind of everyone. 'We need to ask you one thing, even
though we know what you are going to say. We all say that
when asked it.'

Rajiv knows what is coming. 'I know what you are going
to ask. And I will tell you the truth, why should I not? The
truth is, I honestly don't know if I killed him.'

'How is that possible? I've never heard anyone say that!'

'That's the truth. It'd have been easy for me to say I didn't
kill Mihir Kothari. In fact, that's what my lawyer has been
telling the court during all our hearings. But not you guys. You
deserve to know the truth. Because strangers are your best
friends. They want nothing in return. It's like the people you
meet on a train journey. They lend their ears. It doesn't matter
if they are judging you, for they are going to get off at the next
station, and you will never see them again. So it is with all of
you. It doesn't matter what you think of me. And my life story
doesn't matter to you one bit. We are merely passing time. Of
which I have but a month.'

'*Bas kar pagle, ab rulayega kya,*' says the darkness and the cell erupts in laughter once more.

'True,' chips in another voice, 'I didn't cry this much even when my wife left me.' More laughter, which reluctantly subsides as a baton is dragged over the door outside and the metal heel of a boot strikes the hard stone floor of the gangway. Someone is preparing for dawn and the many cruel rituals that accompany it.

* * *

Inspector Apte's shared office at the Mumbai Police headquarters is packed with officers and constables, glued to the TV as it beams live updates of the Rajiv Mehra case. The verdict is to be announced any moment now. As is the custom, many officers have placed bets, and one of them is busy jotting down the names next to the amounts. Chaos ensues as the policemen shout their odds and haggle over the sums they are due if the verdict goes in their favour. Conviction rates don't exactly favour Apte and his efforts, but his colleagues are upbeat. They pass teasing jibes at Apte as he sips his chai and busies himself in clearing his desk. Today, as it happens, is his last day at the office.

'Apte sir, how can you work on your last day?' asks a constable.

'But he isn't,' answers a colleague. 'Clearing a desk is not working. By the way, Apte, what are you going to do with all this case material?'

'Ask Shinde,' replies Apte cheerfully. 'All these files are going to his floor, where they will rot for the next fifty years.'

Shinde laughs. 'Sir, what's next for you? I don't think you are the type to just sit back and do nothing.'

Before Apte can respond, his colleague butts in, 'What do you think our Apte has been doing all his life? Nothing.' The entire office breaks into loud laughter.

'Quiet!' shouts one officer. 'Here comes the verdict.'

All eyes turn to the TV. The reporters and news crews outside the court have gone berserk. Because cameras are not allowed inside the courtroom, the happenings are being relayed to the reporters by their stringers, and this seems to be responsible for the utter confusion wrecking news studios. No one knows the definitive news, but everyone is forced to give the impression that they do. The folks deputed with running the ticker on the screen are having a field day. Acquitted, Convicted, Guilty, Innocent, to be hanged, is being let off—words and phrases gleefully being swapped without a care in the world.

'*Arey ho kya raha hai, bhen chod,*' cries one irate officer. He is shushed by Apte as he flicks the channel to the one he considers to be relatively more reliable. More reliable maybe, but equally ear-splitting. 'The verdict has been announced,' screams the reporter as he jostles for space amid a mass of journalists and TV cameras. 'Guilty!' shouts another. The word 'Guilty!' travels around the horde like a wave.

'Rajiv Mehra has been found guilty of first-degree murder,' continues the reporter. 'In a departure from the norm, the judge has also announced the sentence, which is normally handed out a few days after the verdict. We are now hearing that—' the reporter tilts his head pretending to listen into his earpiece. 'Yes. The sentence is death by hanging. I repeat.

Death by hanging. Rajiv Mehra is condemned to death by hanging. Breaking news. You heard it here first . . .'

The entire office erupts in joy. Apte's colleagues rush to congratulate him and shake his hand and thump his back. He accepts the compliments self-effacingly.

His colleagues demand a party. 'Your last case, Apte, and it is a conviction. Let's cancel the retirement party we had planned for you and have one for this instead,' hollers a colleague.

Apte laughs and closes the lid on the box of files. He smacks his palm over it. 'Thirty-five years in the service, and today it ends with this box.'

But he is not being heard at all. His colleagues are already pushing him through the door to take him to their favourite joint. It is party time.

* * *

It is well after midnight when he walks through the main gate of UDCT (University Department of Chemical Technology), Mumbai. The campus roads are empty, except for a few students strolling about. No one notices him as he makes his way to the chemistry department. He waits to make sure the entrance remains desolate and then strides in. He knows where to go. The CCTV surveillance room is on the first floor at the end of a long corridor, next to the lab from where he stole potassium cyanide.

In the empty room, he gets to work. The CDs are filed by the date they were recorded on. Running his fingers along the stacks, he locates the one he is looking for and inserts it in the laptop he has brought along. He fast-forwards to the date and the time he was here last.

The door swings open. A portly man in his late fifties stands at the entrance. There is a delay, where both men are locked in a stare and lost for words, before the old man takes a step in. 'Who are you? How did you get in?' he asks.

'I was asked by the centralized security to check your CCTV link. They told me there was a problem. Looks fine to me,' says the man, averting his gaze and sliding his laptop inside the backpack, trying to appear casual.

The old man is not convinced. More so when he notices what appears to be a gun inside the partly opened backpack. He turns around and sprints out of the room.

'Shit!' mutters the man under his breath as he springs up from the chair and runs after the old man. But the old man is nowhere to be seen. The corridor is dark and strewn with broken furniture and dusty Godrej almirahs. The man treads down the corridor stealthily and then down the stairway. He enters the basement. It is dark except for the bleak light filtering in through a broken window. There is a sudden shuffling of feet. The old man comes into view. Before he can rush up the steps, there is a wire around his neck. He grabs the wire with both his hands and tries to pull it off his neck, but it is hopeless. A moment later his body writhes and then goes flaccid. The old man is dead.

He has a problem now. What is to be done with the old man's body? This was not in the plan. Glancing about, he notices a long nylon rope tied around a barrel. He removes the rope and flings it over the beam running under the roof. He fashions a lasso with the other end and hangs the old man from the beam. Then he leaves the basement, quickly checking to see that there are no signs of his presence and of the struggle.

Back in the CCTV room, he zips up his backpack. He switches on the desktop and types a brief suicide note, leaving the MS Word window open. At the door, he gives the room a quick once-over, then pulls the door shut gently. He checks his watch. The navy-blue dial of his Rolex glows luminescent in the dim light.

* * *

4

The kitchen has been emptied of its workforce, with the cooks and helpers driven out soon after the evening meal and completion of their shifts. Now the giant kitchen, more a hall in itself, echoes with the guards' laughter and natter; it is ready for Rajiv.

What is your last wish? the superintendent had enquired, gently and politely. The officers and guards have unmistakably gone soft on Rajiv ever since he was handed the capital punishment by the judge. He has been shifted to another ward, with spacious, independent cells and clean, attached toilets. The death row inmates get a fresh change every morning. There is even a cooler in every cell. It is a world away from the cramped, filthy, dangerous, almost unliveable conditions of the general prison ward. The certainty of death elicits an empathy that the uncertainty of life can never manage. It is almost a quasi-religious bequest that humans turn kind towards those destined for the gallows.

'Anything you want,' the superintendent had promised.

'Anything?' Rajiv had asked with a smile.

'Anything that can be requisitioned through a tender,' the warden had chuckled amid generous laughs.

'All right, then,' Rajiv had said. 'I want to cook my last meal myself—nothing exotic, nothing expensive, nothing that is not available, nothing that cannot be requisitioned through a tender, in duplicate if need be.'

A guard clicks open Rajiv's handcuffs and gestures with his arm for Rajiv to proceed. Rubbing his wrists, Rajiv ambles over to the hob. Everything he had asked for from the superintendent is in a cardboard carton on the counter. Meanwhile, the guard lights a bidi and parks himself on a stool a few feet away. 'What are you making?' he asks.

'The last supper,' says Rajiv, knowing the witticism would be lost on the guard.

He takes out the ingredients from the carton. Staring at the Dalda tin, Rajiv smiles. It must have taken the superintendent some effort to acquire this, given that Dalda went out of production years ago. He cuts open the tin, scoops a ladleful of pure trans-fat and smacks it into the kadai. Next, he sieves wheat flour over it, continuing to stir the gooey concoction. *The personification of memory.* That is what has kept him alive this past month. Recollecting all those magical dishes and their recipes, inducing their journey from a sparking neuron in his brain to his taste buds and then back. And today, for this, the most important meal of his life, he has decided to cook what he used to for the Sis Ganj gurdwara langar. Aate ka halwa that, if one were to bunch one's fingers and pick some of it up, it'd slip through and plop down on the pattal; masoor dal, so rich in cream and ghee that even pregnant women in dire need of rich nourishment would think twice; and thick but soft rotis to go along.

Watching Rajiv stir the halwa endlessly with his left hand while getting ready to splosh the tadka on the masoor dal with the other, the guard can't resist the temptation. He gets up and comes over. Rajiv removes a spoonful of the halwa and offers it to the man. The guard gulps it down. It is as though he is transported to another world. 'It's unbelievable,' he says. 'I never thought halwa could taste this good.'

'Halwa is halwa,' he adds, 'what the hell have you put in it?'

'Dalda and memories,' says Rajiv.

It is approaching 10 p.m. when Rajiv is ready with the meal. He asks the guard to inform the superintendent. 'I have a request,' says Rajiv to the superintendent as soon as he enters the kitchen. 'Anything, just say it,' replies the officer.

'Could you deliver this meal to my ex-cellmates?' says Rajiv.

The warden nods. 'You aren't having it?' he asks.

'I already did,' says Rajiv.

'You did? I don't see any plates, any used crockery?'

'I didn't need them. I imagined having the entire meal as I was preparing it.'

The warden understands. He checks his watch and lets some time pass out of politeness and then gestures to the guard, who comes over and handcuffs Rajiv.

The men walk out of the kitchen in silence. As Rajiv enters his cell, he closes his eyes and imagines the meal again. The next moment he retches and rushes to the bathroom, where he vomits his guts out. The warden hands him a tumbler of water. Rajiv thanks him. Had too much to eat, he says.

* * *

Spread before Rohit in all its intimidating grandeur is the Milky Way. It mocks his insignificance, the futility of his very existence. Bewitched, he has been staring at this celestial splendour for a good half hour—that unmistakable gaseous splotch, the twinkling stars, millions of them, combining to furnish an overpowering panorama, unequalled and unmatched by anything made by man or nature. Crickets chirp intermittently in the background, breaking that strange metronomic buzz that rings in the ears and keeps one alert. He repositions his head on the crook of his left arm and renews the stargazing. On impulse, he turns his head to the side and kisses his girlfriend full on the mouth—a deep, lingering kiss. She is surprised but gives in.

'What brought that on?' she asks with a smile. The long kiss was sprinkled at the end with small squirrely ones.

'Nothing,' he says.

Another friend and his girlfriend are lying on their backs a few feet away, also gazing at the stars.

'You want another beer?' Rohit asks, passing them the joint he has just pulled a quick drag from.

'Yes,' they answer in unison.

He dusts himself off and walks to the Land Cruiser parked in the clearing a little distance beyond. Returning with a couple of beer bottles, he flops back on the earth again. 'This is how I want to spend the rest of my life,' he says, taking a swig.

His friend, Aryan, laughs and breaks into a song. '*Akele hain toh kya gum hai . . .*'

'Really, man. I'm serious,' says Rohit, handing Aryan the bottle.

'Shut up,' says Aryan. 'Your dad will give you a nice kick up your backside.'

'I'm eighteen, dude. He can't do anything.'

'Are you even hearing yourself? *Daaru pee, ganja phook, mast reh, aur kal dad ki factory mein timecard punch kar subeh subeh.*'

The girls break into a giggly laugh.

Rohit swears and chucks a pebble at Aryan. It misses him and skips down to the undergrowth by the side, where it distracts a small animal that skittles away. The girls giggle again.

'I am serious, bro,' says Aryan.

'You have it good, bhai. This country is eating me from the inside. No one's keeping an eye on you in the States. You can do as you like.'

'What bull. I am grating my ass off in an investment bank while you sit in your plush office and supervise a team of two hundred men and women polishing diamonds. I am the one who should be complaining. Let's switch our lives.'

'You haven't seen *Jab We Met*? I feel like Shahid Kapoor.'

'Fuck me. Are you saying our Sunaina is Kareena?' jokes one of the girls. 'Hey listen ya,' she adds. 'Are you guys going to keep up with this boring chat or can we go now?'

'Where do you want to go?' asks Rohit, getting up.

'Wherever the road takes us. But fast,' says Niharika.

'Like how fast? *Aaj bata hi do,*' chuckles Aryan, swaying and barely able to stand.

'The fastest you have ever driven,' chips in Sunaina.

'What are you waiting for, then,' cries Rohit, hooking his leather jacket over his shoulder. 'The first to the Cruiser gets to be behind the wheel.'

* * *

It is 3 a.m. It is time. The guard unlocks Rajiv's cell and
switches on the light. Rajiv is sitting on his bed, his hands
pushing down on the mattress, staring blankly at the wall
opposite. He turns his head and smiles. The guard returns
the gesture with a gloomy nod and places the fresh change
of clothes on the bed. Ten minutes, he informs Rajiv politely
and leaves.

The governor slurps his early morning tea in his office,
sunk in his swivel chair, his feet crossed on the table. The only
sound is of the ticking wall clock and of his shoes clapping to
its beat. Under his heels is splayed open a tabloid; the headline
screams, 'Last minute appeal to the President fails; Rajiv
Mehra to be hanged tomorrow at Taloja Prison'. The Arthur
Road hangman is indisposed it appears. Inset is a Google map
snapshot, showing the distance between Arthur Road and
Taloja, as though the journey is an adventure. The hanging is
to be conducted at 5 a.m.

The governor glances at the clock. 3.10 a.m. He springs
from his chair, collects his cane from the table, and strides out
of the office.

Rajiv, surrounded by armed guards, his wrists shackled
behind his back, struggles through the long hallway that
will lead them to the open yard where his transport is
waiting. His has vomited twice already. His stomach is
churning. He feels drained, exhausted. He wants to slump
to the floor. *Why the formality? Kill me here and now, save yourselves
the trouble*, he is thinking. Myriad thoughts enter his mind.
His past flashes before his eyes. He wants none of it. His
future has never been more certain. He knows it. He has
seen it. It cannot be changed. If only he could die with the
snap of his fingers.

The cells in the hallway are dark. The prisoners are fast asleep. Rajiv plods on, determined to put on a brave face, his bloodshot eyes fixed on the distance.

A Scorpio is waiting, with police vans on either side of it. The governor swings round at the sound of Rajiv and the guards approaching. Ignitions are turned on, engines gun to life and the rickety chassis of the two vans rattle. Rajiv is brought to a halt before the governor. He looks up. The governor nods. Armed policemen take their allotted seats in the vehicles. Rajiv is unshackled and then shackled again but with his arms now in front. He is pushed inside on to the back seat of the Scorpio. A policeman climbs in after him. The doors are shut and locked. The boom barrier lifts, and they are on their way. The convoy speeds past empty Mumbai streets. Rajiv has a little less than two hours left in this world.

* * *

'Woo-hoo!' screams Aryan, emerging through the sunroof as the Land Cruiser zips on the Sion–Panvel expressway. He punches the air in a state of frenzy and takes a swig from a beer bottle. 'Awesome!' he exults and ducks inside the cabin, exchanging the beer bottle for a joint that Rohit, in the driver's seat, passes to him. The two girls in the back giggle away and complain the car isn't going fast enough. Rohit scoffs and steps on the gas. More hooting and wolf whistling follows as the Cruiser swerves perilously on hilly turns.

* * *

Rajiv hasn't uttered a word since they left Arthur Road. He is thankful for the silence inside the Scorpio. Even the policemen know when to be solemn. The convoy slows down as they approach the Vashi bridge toll plaza. The driver lights a cigarette and lowers the window. Rajiv is thankful for the fresh air that wafts in.

The convoy picks up speed again as it passes the toll. The highway is free of traffic except for a few lorries that come hurtling past blaring their musical horns. The cars slow down as the Sion expressway narrows, slicing through Kharghar forest, with the dual carriageway turning single and the road snaking up the hill. Rajiv looks out of the window to his right. Only the outlines of the ravine and the trees carpeting it are discernible in the moonlight. The shimmering waters of the river below appear and disappear as the car winds through the hairpin turns. He closes his eyes.

* * *

The setting is out of this world. The 236-metre-tall Skylon Tower Revolving Dining Room, which overlooks Niagara Falls, is in the middle of pampering its most famous guest ever—the Queen of England. Rumour has it that she and Prince Philip are fans of Indian cuisine; the official word used is 'enchanted'. The restaurant has laid out a twelve-course dinner in her honour. And who else to have prepared it but the most famous chef in the world, Rajiv Mehra.

Soft music plays as the guests mingle inside the revolving restaurant—the Canadian prime minister has just struck his champagne glass and pleaded for some quiet. The Queen is being introduced to the chefs and their staff. She runs quickly through the line and then stops to chat with Rajiv. 'I have never had Indian food that tastes this good,' she tells him. Prince Philip chimes in. 'That was astonishing, young man. You have a standing invitation to visit Buckingham Palace and teach our lot a few tricks,' he jokes. Rajiv thanks the couple and bends his knee a touch as the Queen offers him her delicate hand. A run of protocols later, with the royal entourage having departed, Rajiv is mobbed by his staff and fellow chefs. They want to hear every word that the Queen said to him.

Embarrassed, blushing even, Rajiv heads off to a corner where he can be by himself and gather his breath. But there is little hope of that tonight. 'Congratulations, Rajiv, you were awesome.' Rajiv turns around, forsaking the spectacular view of Niagara Falls for a moment. It is Juliet Cresson, the French Michelin-star chef. Rajiv accepts the compliment with a bow of his head and thanks her. But Juliet is in no mood to chat or exchange pleasantries. Before Rajiv can react, he is kissed full on the lips. Rajiv yields. Juliet peels away and stares achingly into Rajiv's eyes. She proceeds to kiss him again, this time longer and hungrier, and Rajiv doesn't want it to end and the pleasure is coming in waves and he presses Juliet against the glass wall and her hands grab his buttocks and his palms cup her cheeks and their . . .

Rajiv jolts back with a violent shudder. A truck has just passed them by, its horn piercing a shrill tune through the stillness of the early morning. The Scorpio's driver curses extendedly while the others in the cabin laugh, both at him and at Rajiv. 'Were you dreaming?' they ask him. Rajiv shakes his head, mortified, and looks out of the window.

* * *

The teenager cranes his neck up, relishing the wind battering his face, his locks flowing back like the flames of a fire. He sucks in another drag from his joint and stares at the dark road ahead that their Cruiser is gobbling up faster and faster, the vertical cliff face on one side of it illuminated by the high beam. And then he sees the police van. He screams in reflex. But it is too late.

The driver of the police van blows his horn and veers to the left, ramming head-on into the cliff face. The Scorpio following behind veers to the right and is hit frontally on the passenger side, lifting it clean off the road. It cartwheels in the air a couple of times and plunges down the ravine into the river below. It enters the water vertically, like a diver would, and continues to descend, losing its momentum with every passing second, until it settles, vertical, on the riverbed. It bounces off sluggishly, only to settle back on the bed again, but this time on its wheels. There it is, as though on display in a showroom, except that it is on a riverbed, with water all around it. The cabin is miraculously still lit up and so are the headlights.

The three policemen and the driver are dead. Rajiv is bleeding heavily from the forehead, with the two dead policemen on top of him. Water has begun to seep into the cabin, slowly at first and then with force. Rajiv opens his eyes, horror-struck. He wants to close them again but the animal instinct to survive takes over. He pushes away the bodies and extracts the keys to the handcuffs from the pocket of one of the dead policemen. He removes his handcuffs and hunts for something to break the window with. Time is running out. The water has reached his neck. There is but a sliver of space between the cabin roof and the water level, and it is only a matter of seconds before his head goes under.

Rajiv swallows in a lungful of air and slithers across to the front seats. Frantically searching the dead policeman's body, he manages to grab hold of the revolver. He unbuttons the holster and removes the gun. It slips from his grasp. The cabin lights and the headlights go dead. Rajiv is enveloped by total darkness. The only sound is of the rushing water outside. With not a moment to lose, he crouches down and sweeps the floor blind with his hands to locate the gun. It is stuck underneath the driver's seat. Air has begun to escape from his mouth in the form of giant bubbles. He manages to free the gun at last. He straightens and gets a good grip. He cannot see the windows or the windshield, surrounded as he is by darkness. He fires, multiple times. The window smashes. Clutching the sides of the window, Rajiv manages to extricate himself from the cabin. A moment later he surfaces above the water, the force of the river taking him downstream at great speed.

He thrashes his arms and swallows lungful of air. The river is taking a turn; he can sense it, even in the darkness and with his head bobbing up and down in the violent current. The river is smooth and level now, almost by magic. The torrent has disappeared. Something is not right. And then he hears it—the sound of the colossal Pandavkada waterfall he is about to vanish into. Before he can react, he finds himself tumbling down the cascade and into the river below. He tries to grab at something—a rock, a tree branch, anything—but he can't. The speed of the river is immense. Helpless, Rajiv slackens his muscles and leaves himself to the mercy of the current. He is hurtling down at great speed when his descent is halted. Miraculously, his body is wedged between two rock faces splitting the water. He is beyond feeling any pain now, just thankful that he is breathing. He manages to swim ashore, collapsing on the riverbank. He turns his body face up. He stares blankly at the sky above and the Milky Way.

He is alive. He checks his watch. It is 5 a.m., the exact time he was to be hanged.

* * *

Click. The alarm rings, its shrillness an assault on the senses. Inspector Apte slaps the clock in anger and tosses and turns in the bed. His wife is next to him and snoring merrily. He switches on the table lamp and staggers out of the bedroom. Dawn is breaking, but it is still gloomy. He opens the main door and picks up the milk bottle and the newspaper and goes to the kitchen to boil the milk, switching the TV on along the way.

Leaning against the kitchen wall, he is watching the milk boil with droopy eyes when he is shocked into attention by the TV in the living room. There has been an accident on the Sion highway. The anchor is screaming at the top of his voice as he recounts the details. Rajiv Mehra is dead, he declares, rather grandly, caring little for propriety. Apte jolts out of his stupor and rushes to the living room. The shaky visuals just about manage to capture the deep ravine and the river flowing below.

'Five policemen are dead. Four of them were in the vehicle that was transporting Rajiv Mehra to Taloja. The home minister has just arrived at the scene,' hams the reporter, trying his level best not to lose his footing as he descends the perilous slope. 'The Scorpio they were travelling in fell into the river. None of the bodies have been found. The Scorpio too has not been located. A search and rescue mission is underway.'

Inspector Apte is stunned. He stares blankly at the TV screen, the milk forgotten. He can see, from the lit-up display, that his phone is ringing, even though it is on the table a good distance away. Finally, he strides over and picks it up. It is Tukaram.

'Have you heard, sir?' asks Tukaram with childlike excitement.

'Yes. The TV is in front of me,' says Apte collectedly.

'The commissioner has ordered us to assemble at the HQ.'

'Why are you telling me this, Tukaram? I retired. Or didn't you know?'

'Sorry, sir. I just thought . . .'

'Thought what?'

'I just thought you'd like to know, that's all. Rajiv Mehra is dead.'

'Well, he was being taken to Taloja to be hanged anyway, was he not?'

'Yes, sir.'

'Have they found his body yet?'

'No, sir. But he's dead.'

'How do you know that? You are watching the same channel as I am right now, I take it?'

'Ganesh just called me, sir. He told me Rajiv is dead. That's why the commissioner has called us.'

'Well, anyhow. Good luck.'

'Thank you, sir. Is there anything you can tell me that might help me? This is a good chance for me. A promotion might be in the offing.'

The reason for the call is becoming clearer now. 'Hold your horses right there, Tukaram. Help you how?' he asks.

'Nothing, sir. I just thought you might know something that we don't.'

'I don't know where you are going with this, Tukaram,' says Apte, now clearly irritated. 'Wherever you are, drop it. My milk has boiled over. I need to go.'

Having disconnected the call, Apte returns to the kitchen to clean up the hob, thinking of Rajiv Mehra. 'I worked my pants off for a month just so he could hang,' he mutters to himself, 'but the bastard couldn't even do that for me.'

* * *

Rajiv has been on foot for the best part of an hour. He has a limp, a severely bruised ankle and an open wound on the side of his head, but other than that, he is fine. The forest that he has just traversed was tight and unforgiving. His clothes are soaking wet and covered with thorns and twigs and leaves. He has arrived at a clearing. In the distance is an ancient temple, half in ruins. Rajiv hobbles towards it and collapses by the shallow steps.

The first rays of the sun arrive. It is serene and still. He bends his knees and puts his head between them. This is his end. He wonders why he tried to save himself. A reflex, he reasons; man can't forsake hope. Suicide or losing the will to live cannot be thrust upon him unexpectedly—it has to be arrived at rationally. The same Rajiv who was calm and had resigned himself to the thought of his life being snatched away from him, had, inside that fast-sinking Scorpio, tried his best to live. 'But that is not the case now,' he says to himself. 'I have my wits restored. I can think rationally now. And there is no point in living any more. This is the end; the last hour of my life.'

All of a sudden, the temple resounds with a thundering rendition of the Tandav Stotram. Rajiv looks up. A bare-chested sadhu, his arms raised to the skies, is standing opposite a giant Shiva linga and beseeching the god. His chanting is hypnotic. Rajiv can't recall when he last saw something so elemental, so overpowering. The sadhu's eyes are closed, and it is as though he has become his own judge—cruel, merciless, the destroyer of his vanity—as he invokes the Destroyer of the World himself. With every rising note, Rajiv gets the feeling that the stone is coming to life, trembling, quivering like the voice before it; the stone is listening—how can it not?

Jata tavi gala jala pravaha pavi tasthale
Gale valambya lambitam bhujanga tunga malikam
Damad damad damad damad ninada vada marvayam
Chakara chand tandavam tano tunah shivah shivam

Rajiv's life flashes before his eyes. The futility of it, its worthlessness—that was apparent to him a minute before, these thoughts have turned into smoke and are drifting away.

Jata kata hasam bhrama bhramani limpa nirjhari
Vilo lavichi valari viraja mana murdhani
Dhaga dhaga dhaga jjva lala lata patta pavake
Kishora Chandra shekhare ratih pratikshanam mama

'What is guilt?' asks Rajiv. 'Something that is thrust upon you, or something that grows within you? If the latter, then is it not like love that can create as well as destroy you? What is the difference between the two anyway, when there is a god that creates, and accompanying him is a god that destroys?'

Dhara dharendra nandini vilasa bandhu bandhuras
Phura diganta santati pramoda mana manase
Krupa kataksha dhorani nirudha durdha rapadi
Kvachi digambare mano vinodametu vastuni

'Why should I not live till I am destined to? What is consciousness? Can it be thrust upon me? Am I guilty? Can others proclaim me guilty if I myself do not know if I am guilty? Why did I try and save myself when I could so easily have succumbed to the elements and breathed my last under water? Why did I fight with every last sinew of my being?'

Jata bhujanga pingala sphurat phana maniprabha
Kadamba kunkuma drava pralipta digva dhumukhe
Madandha sindhu rasphuratva guttariya medure
Mano vinoda madbhutam bibhartu bhuta bhartari

The sadhu's arms jab the air above as he enters a trance, invoking and imploring his lord. The stone is going to respond, thinks *Rajiv. It is! There is life in it. Then why should I want to extinguish the life within me?*

Sahastra lochana prabhitya sheshalekha shekhara
Prasuna dhuli dhorani vidhusa ranghri pithabhuh
Bhujangaraja malaya nibaddha jata jutaka
Shriyai chiraya jayatam chakora bandhu shekharah

I am not guilty of any crime. I did not kill the man I loved and admired. It will all come back to me, the truth. I am pure, says Rajiv, this time out loud. The sadhu's rendition of the Tandav

Stotram has reached inconceivable heights. His matted locks are flying in all directions. The ash from his face and chest is puffing up and floating out, the particles catching the first rays of the sun and glittering like tinsel, forming a hallow around his body. I want to live, says Rajiv.

Lalata chatva rajvala dhanajnjayas phulingabha
nipita pancha sayakam naman nilim panayakam
Sudha mayukhale khaya viraja manashekharam
Maha kapali sampade shiroja talamastunah

I did not kill Mihir. All that evidence was news to me. There is more than one truth. There is their truth, and there is mine. Where is my truth? So what if I cannot remember it right now? I will find it!

Karala bhala pattika dhagad dhagad dhagad jjvala
Ddhanajnjaya hutikruta prachanda pancha sayake
Dhara dharendra nandini kuchagra chitrapatraka
Prakalpa naika shilpini trilochane ratir mama

I will find the truth come what may. I will live for it. I am not done. I am not finished. I am not dead!

navina megha mandali niruddha dur dharas phurat
Kuhuni sheetini tamah prabandha baddha kandharah
nilimpa nirjhari dhara stanotu krutti sindhurah
Kalani dhana bandhurah shriyam jagad dhuran dharah

The tempo surges to a dreamlike level as the sadhu's words echo in the temple. The verses seem to multiply. The hypnosis is near complete.

Praphulla nila pankaja prapajncha kalimchatha
Vdambi kantha kandali ruchiprabaddha kandharam
Smarachchidam purachchhidam bhavachchidam makhachchidam
Gajachchidandha kachidam tamam takachchidam bhaje

Rajiv smothers his face with his hand. He is ready.

Akharva sarva mangala kala kadamba majnjari
Rasa pravaha madhuri vijrumbhana madhu vratam
Smarantakam purantakam bhavantakam makhantakam
Gajantakandha kantakam tamanta kantakam bhaje

And then, just as suddenly as the sadhu began the chant, he ends it. The last word that escapes his mouth lingers on for an eternity, its syllables floating in the air and breaking into a million atoms that permeate every living and non-living thing in the vicinity.

Silence descends once more. The sadhu turns around and slips his feet into his *khadaun*. He climbs down the steps and passes Rajiv cowering inside the stone lair adjacent. Rajiv has the sudden urge to call after him, but he resists. The sadhu keeps walking and disappears into the forest.

The wind has stopped blowing. The sun is up. Rajiv is by himself. He gets up. He knows what is to be done.

* * *

5

Gurmukh Singh Talwar, a middle-aged man, his cheeks ravaged by smallpox, his belly straining his shirt buttons, enters the Mumbai Police headquarters, and keeping his head lowered at all times, takes the staircase to the floor that houses the evidence and documentation department.

The office is large and busy, staff and researchers going about their business. No one pays him any attention. On one side of the bureau is a row of cubicles and on the other side, a mad arrangement of numbered and lettered Godrej almirahs, their tops laden with dusty files kissing the ceiling. The office opens into a high-ceilinged hall that is the research and library space, with crudely partitioned tables holding antique desktops. A large Xerox machine occupies one corner, a water-cooler the other. The Xerox is humming and churning constantly.

Gurmukh locates the cubicle that houses the department head, Sub Inspector Satyasivam Nair. The policeman is slurping on his tea while reading a newspaper. The office might be buzzing with activity, but it is a quiet day for Nair.

It always is. Gurmukh knocks on the partition. 'Good morning, sir. I am Gurmukh Singh Talwar. Can I talk to you for five minutes?'

Nair looks up from the newspaper, just the top half of his face visible, and slides his glasses down his nose like a magistrate; the manoeuvre is obviously well practised. 'What do you want?' he asks, scanning Gurmukh from head to toe.

'I am from the chief production team of Netflix,' says Gurmukh deferentially, handing Nair his visiting card. 'We are making a documentary web series on the Kothari murder case. We would like to requisition all the CCTV footage concerning the case, in particular the footage from the Taaj.'

Nair scoffs, giving the impression Gurmukh has said something outlandish. 'You are talking of days of footage, probably more,' he says disinterestedly, about to return to his newspaper. 'And besides, you will have to watch it here, then mark out the segments you need for your documentary so that we can get a copy made of just those portions.'

'When can I start, sir?' says Gurmukh.

The eagerness surprises Nair. But he is as hard-boiled as they come. 'If you want a copy of the footage, you will have to fill up a requisition form. Approval will take a month if you are lucky. You can fill in this other form, here, for requesting an in-person visit to come and screen the footage here. It might take a week, maybe two. And now, if you don't mind, I am busy.'

Gurmukh nods his appreciation. 'Thank you, sir. Can the process not be speeded up?' he asks, then adds, trying his best to soften up Nair, 'We will also need to interview police officers. And if you are free, perhaps we could interview you, too.'

Nair's face lights up. Gurmukh smiles and carries on, encouraged. 'There is massive interest in the case, as you can imagine. We would like to film and air the web series as soon as possible. This is the right moment for it.'

'Good. Good,' says Nair, now taking an interest in the conversation. 'But I didn't have anything to do with the case. I have just been transferred here from Chennai last week. You would need to talk to the officers who handled the case. I could get you in touch with them.'

'That would be great, sir,' says Gurmukh, 'Just what we want. And needless to say, there will be a small token of appreciation from our side for any help you render. An honorarium, if you will.'

Nair smirks but tries to appear nonchalant. 'Someone I knew long ago actually handled this case. Inspector Apte. But he has since retired.'

'Oh, we have contacted Inspector Apte already. He was very forthcoming. He agreed to be interviewed,' says Gurmukh. The tone is now conversational and relaxed. 'We can interview you too, as his friend and colleague. But only if you agree.'

Nair tries hard to hide his glee. 'Yes, I won't mind.'

'Done. We typically pay one lakh for a ten-minute interview,' says Gurmukh.

Nair wants to smack the table in delight but restrains himself. 'Money doesn't matter. Telling the truth does.'

Gurmukh suppresses a grin. 'So, when can I inspect the footage? I hope you understand time is of the essence. Already many other production houses are planning to make similar documentaries, and—'

Nair thrusts a form at Gukmukh even before the latter has finished his sentence. 'Here, you fill this up. Don't worry;

normally it would take two weeks or more, but I will expedite the process. Come after two days. You will be able to examine the footage. And fill this second form too while you are at it. We'll try and get the copy request accepted along with.'

'Thank you, Mr Nair,' smiles Gurmukh. 'This is great. You have been very helpful. I'll come back in two days then?'

'Yes,' says Nair. His stare lingers for longer than required. Gurmukh understands. 'And when I am here on Friday, we can discuss your interview as well as monetary compensation for all your help. In fact, I will bring a small token as advance. Can't thank you enough.'

'Oh, don't mention it,' says Nair with a grin. 'See you on Friday.'

Gurmukh gets up and exits Nair's cubicle. Outside, he finds the entire office has magically emptied. He checks his Rolex. It must be lunchtime.

* * *

His head leans against the rusted window bars of a rickety bus that is packed to the rafters. His body shakes and judders with every movement the bus makes as it traverses through *kutcha* countryside roads. But he is indifferent. Nothing fazes him. He tightens the ragged shawl round his chest and continues to gaze at the dusty sunset.

Rajiv is on the road to nowhere. He carries no luggage, no money and no expectation. He gets off and boards a bus wherever he wants, on a whim; sometimes he walks long distances on village roads, cuts through dense forests, crosses hip-deep rivers, as though they were all hands of a clock, passing, sweeping, unconcerned with the ways of the world, inevitable, relentless. He sleeps on park benches and at railway platforms of mofussil towns. When it rains, he takes shelter under a bridge or a shop awning or in a temple courtyard. Sometimes he boards a bus, sometimes a train; and sometimes lorry drivers take pity on him and give him a lift. He eats at roadside dhabas, and if asked to pay, he pays in kind by doing the dishes or sweeping the floor. He hasn't read a newspaper or watched TV or heard the radio for a week. He doesn't know what is happening around him or in the country or the world. He has reduced human existence to its basics. He is enduring. He is surviving. He is a bunch of cells rolling, progressing, advancing to their logical finish—death. And this is his catharsis, his way of purging his body and mind of a lifetime of poison and toxicity in the form of dreams and aspirations and the daily grind.

Today, on a whim, he has decided to travel to Varanasi, the abode of the lord who saved him a week ago from wilfully ending his life. He is on an overcrowded train, down on his haunches by the open door, his body moving from side to side like a car-wiper, the wind rustling through hair that is now matted and dreadlocked, and a salt and pepper beard that has grown thick. He does not know the time and neither does he care. He is going to the city named after the one who transcends it. Mahakaal.

The train comes to a halt at Varanasi junction with a backward tug. Coolies stream in and there is immense pushing and shoving. Rajiv gets down. He has the appearance of a sadhu. His gait is of the kind attained once you spurn all desires. And it exudes a certain confidence. People give way, they bow, show respect; he walks by without displaying any acknowledgement. He exits the station and mills among the crowd on the street.

To quench his thirst, he stops by a roadside *pyau*. Hungry, he enters a Vaishnav dhaba and informs the proprietor how he is going to pay for his bill. When the owner nods, he steps outside where the halwai is frying kachoris and returns with half a dozen wrapped in a newspaper. He eats, without pleasure or zeal, and when he has had his fill, he raises a tumbler over his tilted face and pours water into his mouth. His eyes fall on the newspaper the kachoris were wrapped in. Normally, he wouldn't have paid much attention, but the headline distracts him. It concerns the Sion accident. The report informs that the police have finally retrieved the Scorpio and all the bodies from it. Four of them were of the policemen and the fifth of the chef Rajiv Mehra. The policemen were in their uniforms; Rajiv Mehra was in handcuffs. The bodies were disfigured and bloated beyond recognition and had to be identified by DNA. The accompanying image is of the five bodies arranged in a row, covered in white sheets. The inset is of Commissioner Singh giving out the details at a press conference, declaring that the case is now closed.

Rajiv realizes abruptly that he is still holding the tumbler raised in the air, while his eyes have been glued to newspaper report. He thumps it back on the table, gets up, crumples the newspaper and walks inside the kitchen to clean the dishes.

* * *

Inspector Apte has been staring at the abstract painting on the opposite wall for ten minutes. He had begun the exercise of trying to decipher it, but along the way he gave way to idling, and is now lost in his thoughts. Truth be told, he is bored. It has been two weeks since he took up his new job at a major BPO as the chief security officer. His office is on the seventh floor of a high-rise, a carpet to ceiling glass-panelled space from where he has a panoramic view of the city. But there is no work. He comes in the morning, he stays on till the evening, and then he leaves for home. The salary is great and so are the people—mostly half his age—but the only excitement he encounters on a daily basis is trying to decode the hidden meaning behind the abstract painting hung on his office wall. He has already taken his tour of the offices, handed out tasks to his subordinates, convened his daily briefing with the CTO, had his lunch—on his own in his office—gulped down three cups of coffee and stared at the painting for an hour. The silence in the office is another form of torture; there is no ceiling fan, no rats scuttling behind stacks of files—there are no files. He wishes he was elsewhere.

The desk phone shatters the silence. Apte springs to pick it up, then corrects his over-exuberance even though no one is watching.

'Is this Inspector Apte?' asks a gruff voice.

'Yes, this is him,' replies Apte clearing his throat.

It is Satyasivam Nair at the other end. Apte takes a few moments to place him. 'Hello, Nair. It's been years, probably ten.'

'Yes, sir,' replies Nair enthusiastically. 'I am now in Mumbai. Transferred from Chennai. Got to know that you have retired. Was sorry to hear that. Would have been nice to catch up. I fondly recall our days in the Academy.'

'Yes, indeed.' Inspector Apte doesn't know where this is going. He maintains a polite silence, hoping all will be revealed shortly—whether it is a courtesy call or one to ask a favour.

'Anyway, sir,' continues Nair, 'I just thought to touch base with you, especially as your name cropped up a few days ago. I should have called you up earlier, but I have been so busy.'

'Which department are you handling, Nair?'

'Evidence and documentation, sir.'

Busy indeed, says Apte to himself with a smirk. 'Good, good. Listen, Nair, we must meet up soon. I have to go now as something's come up. The new job is as hectic as can be.' Apte smirks again, self-deprecatingly, seeing the irony of it.

'Sure, sir,' says Nair. 'I only called to take a few tips from a senior.'

'Regarding what?' asks Apte.

'The interview for the Netflix documentary, sir.'

Apte is bemused. 'Say that again?'

'The Netflix documentary,' repeats Nair. 'Looks like I am also going to be interviewed.'

Apte wants to express his surprise but resists, years of practice and police training coming to his rescue. He waits for Nair to explain further.

'The producer was here last Wednesday, requesting to have a look at the CCTV feed concerning the Kothari case,' says Nair. 'They are making a web series. He said he had had a talk with you already and you had agreed to be interviewed. Then he said even I might be interviewed. Well, I have never done this sort of thing, and so I thought I'd call you up and get some tips.'

'Nice. What was the name of this producer?' asks Apte.

'Gurmukh Singh Talwar. In fact, he is here right now. Scanning the whole footage. He'll be requesting a copy of the relevant portions after he's done. I am processing the paperwork already. I thought I'd expedite it, given that you are also involved.'

'Oh, yes. Gurmukh,' says Apte stretching the name. 'I have misplaced his number. You wouldn't happen to have it on you, would you, Nair?'

'One moment, sir.' Nair shuffles some papers on his desk and finds the visiting card with Gurmukh's number. He repeats it to Apte.

'Thanks, Nair. And listen, it was great catching up with you. Let's meet up soon,' says Apte and with an affable goodbye replaces the receiver. He picks up the receiver again and dials Gurmukh's number.

'Central production team, Netflix, India. How may I help you?' answers a cheerful female voice.

'Yes. I would like to speak with Gurmukh Singh Talwar,' says Apte in an official tone.

'I am sorry, sir, but he is out. He won't be back till late evening,' replies the woman.

'Please give me his mobile number,' says Apte. It is not a request but an order and the woman senses it.

'I am sorry, sir, but I am not allowed to share personal numbers,' she says.

'This is Inspector Dayanand Apte from the Mumbai Police headquarters. Please give me his number. It is urgent,' says Apte.

The woman provides the number straightaway.

'Thank you,' says Apte. 'May I know where he is right now?'

'On a shoot location with his unit. Mumbai–Pune Expressway,' answers the woman.

Apte disconnects the phone, keeping his finger pressed on the button while he ponders his next move. He dials Gurmukh's number.

The library and research wing inside the documentation department resounds with the Teri Mitti ring tone. Staff and researchers look around and eye each other, miffed. The portly man screening the CCTV footage on a desktop, noting down time codes and durations as he goes forward and back on the visuals, is distracted too. He turns his head to investigate. A woman seated two tables away from him is rummaging through her purse, trying to find her phone. She finally manages to do so and swipes to answer the call. Her tone and demeanour suggest it is her boyfriend. Everyone, including the Sikh, returns to their work.

Meanwhile, Gurmukh answers Apte's call, on the sets. 'Yes?'

'Is this Gurmukh Singh Talwar?' asks Apte.

'Yes, this is Gurmukh,' comes the reply.

'I am calling as part of a routine Mumbai Police enquiry,' says Apte. 'Where are you right now?'

There is a moment's delay as Gurmukh lets a speeding lorry pass by. 'Right in the middle of a shoot. On the Mumbai– Pune Expressway. Can I be contacted later?'

'Sure,' says Apte and disconnects. His palms are sweating. He stares at the abstract painting, contemplating his next move. He dials the Mumbai Police HQ switch room. 'This is Apte,' he says. 'Quick. Give me Nair at the evidence department.'

Inside the evidence department's research wing, the Sikh is gathering his stuff and putting it in his bag. His work is done. He has been busy the past hour sketching a map of his surroundings, complete with where the fire escape and the air-conditioning ducts are, to where the CCTV footage and files are arranged serially and stored. He switches off the desktop and pushes the chair back and rises, slinging the backpack over his shoulder.

Apte has abandoned his chair and is pacing the distance allowed to him by the spiral phone cord. 'Nair?' he says in a calm tone. Inside, his heart is beating wildly. 'Is Gurmukh still in the office?'

'Yes, sir, he is; in the research room. I only left him there. Why?' asks Nair confused.

'Make sure he stays put,' says Apte. 'In fact, go to him and tell him to wait; I'd like to see him. Call me from your mobile when you are with him.'

'But—?' asks Nair.

'Just do it. I am disconnecting,' says Apte and bangs the receiver down. He is panting. The back of his neck is damp with sweat. He rubs it with his palm and taps the table. Seconds pass. 'C'mon, Nair,' he mumbles. 'C'mon, damn it!'

The phone rings. Apte picks up the receiver in a flash. It is Nair. There is an uncomfortable silence at the other end, broken by a gentle, nervous cough and clearing of the throat. 'I am sorry, sir,' says Nair. 'Gurmukh is no longer here. He must have slipped out. I don't know when. I was right here in my cubicle all the time this past hour. Sir, if I can ask, why do you want to . . . sir? Hello?'

But Inspector Apte is no longer at the other end, having flung the receiver against the wall and sprinted out of his office.

* * *

Rajiv has been walking the streets of Varanasi aimlessly, blending in with the crowds and the chaos. Temple bells and Vedic chants mix with the azaan and the noises of horns and hawkers to furnish a cacophony that is strangely calming.

He has arrived at the Manikarnika ghat without realizing it. Fate has dealt him this irony. The cremation ground is busy as it is approaching dusk. Lights are coming on. Devotees pass Rajiv by and bow to him, some touch his feet; Rajiv walks on, unconcerned. A guide nearby is explaining the history of the ghat to his flock of foreign tourists. Rajiv sits down on the shallow steps and gazes at the Ganga and the boats sailing past. This is the oldest ghat in Kashi, explains the guide. It is the most sacred ghat. Life and death merge here. Death is celebrated as it gives way to life again. Sati Mata immolated herself here and Lord Shiva, angry and beset with grief, carried her burning body to Kailasa. To make Lord Shiva forget his grief, Lord Vishnu let loose the sudarshan chakra to slice and sever Sati's burning body. Pieces of her body fell to the earth at fifty-one places. These are the fifty-one shaktipeeths. By the time Lord Shiva reached Kailasa, only the head of Sati was left in his arms. He was inconsolable. His third eye opened.

Placing the head of Sati on a rock, he performed the tandav for the first time. He was intent on destroying not only the world but also his city, Kashi. Vexed, Lord Vishnu pleaded with Shiva to spare Kashi, because if Kashi were destroyed, so too would be the nature of time itself. No one would know when to enter the cycle of birth and when to exit it. But Lord Shiva would have none of it. He continued to perform the tandav. Galaxies merged and exploded all around, the sun was eclipsed, the Earth started to burn.

The universe was in danger of being destroyed to smithereens. The end was nigh.

The frightened Vishnu went running to Lord Brahma, the creator of the universe. Together they came up with a solution. They told Lord Shiva to spare Kashi as whoever was cremated where Sati Mata's earring and ear had fallen would attain moksha. The destruction therefore could never be completed. Lord Shiva was pacified; he calmed down, and thus were the universe and Kashi saved.

You are standing right where Sati Mata's earring fell, says the guide to the spellbound tourists. Rajiv, listening in and enthralled by the guide's narration, knows what to do. He is going to spend the rest of his life here, at the Manikarnika ghat. The guide is meanwhile manoeuvring his flock to the famous Satua Baba Ashram at the ghat. Rajiv gets up, dusts himself off and joins the tourist group.

* * *

'Just look straight into the camera and state the facts,' advises Inspector Apte. Satyasivam Nair is listening intently. They are in Nair's cubicle, enjoying masala chai and biscuits and discussing the Netflix documentary. The office has emptied— it is just past 5.30 p.m.—though there are still a few people inside the research and library room.

Inspector Apte has other designs, and he needs to prepare the ground for them. The frustration, though, is building. Nair is behaving like a kid anticipating his first trip to the zoo; inquisitive and bubbly and charged up.

'Sir, for you it may be easy but not for me,' says Nair. 'I have never been in front of the camera.'

'A face like yours should be in Bollywood,' declares Apte. Nair throws his head back and laughs. Apte judges this to be the moment. '*Achcha, suno*, Nair,' he says.

Nair tilts his face attentively. 'Ji, sir.'

'All this while we have been talking about tips for you, but even I need to brush up for the interview,' says Apte. 'It's been a while since I was in the thick of things, what with retirement and all that came along with it. I need to be on my toes as well.'

Nair shakes his head disbelievingly. 'C'mon, sir. You are an encyclopaedia.'

'I am serious, Nair,' continues Apte. I need to go through the evidence again; and nothing better than to kick off with the CCTV footage. I need to go through it, even if it is just to skim over. I can mark out the portions and watch them at length later. So, when can I start?'

'You tell me, sir,' says Nair, impressed by Apte's attention to detail and professionalism.

'Right now, if it's all right with you,' says Apte. 'I am free tonight, but it'll be tough tomorrow onwards. The new job is demanding.'

Nair nods. 'Sure, sir. The research room is all yours. Only issue is, I need to be somewhere else this evening or the wife is going to kill me.'

'You go right ahead. I like working alone anyway.'

'Thank you, sir. But I will ask someone to be here, at your command. How long do you plan to take, sir?'

'Don't know. But I have no other plans so this is it.'

'Sure, sir, no problem. I'll ask Raut to bring you some dinner as well.'

'Thanks, Nair,' says Inspector Apte, getting up. 'I'll leave you to your evening plans. Let's catch up again soon.'

They shake hands. Nair rings the desk bell. A man in a police uniform appears out of nowhere. Nair shouts instructions to him. 'Raut, see to it that Inspector Apte is looked after. He is going to be in the research room for the next few hours.'

That was managed slickly, smiles Apte to himself as he leaves Nair's cubicle; nice and smoothly does it. He is enjoying this.

* * *

The Kothari clan is gathered round the dining table at their family home. The matriarch Miraben, wife of the late Mohanbhai Kothari and mother to Mihir and Rupesh, is at the head, flanked by younger members of the family. Rupesh is at the opposite end. The mood is solemn, as it has been for the past month. Neelima Kothari Thapar is conversing in hushed tones with Rohan, the late Mihir Kothari's son. One chair has been thoughtfully left empty. Mihir's wife, Vrinda, is seated next to it. She sniffles from time to time and Neelima pats and gently squeezes her shoulder. The meal is being had in near silence.

Miraben Kothari clears her throat. Squeezing Rohan's hand lightly as a mark of affection and support, she asks for attention. 'Rupesh,' she says, 'I would like Rohan to take over defence and insurance. There is too much on your plate. I want you to focus on refining and telecom.'

This is the first Rupesh has heard of it. He gets along well with his nephew Rohan, and it was in his mind too, to involve Rohan more in the family business, but he had resisted the urge to announce it so soon. Rohan is in the middle of completing his MBA from Wharton, but he won't be returning to complete it now, given the tragic events. Nonetheless, it would have been asking too much of him to take over extra responsibility. But he resists saying this out loud to his mother, maintaining a stoic silence.

Miraben pats Rohan's hand. She shifts her gaze to Neelima. 'And Neelima should handle beauty products and fashion.'

Neelima nods and tries hard not to show her disappointment. She had thought she'd get telecom, given that she had been handling that sector for the Kothari Group. But, as has always been the case in the Kothari dynasty, elders propose, elders dispose.

'Pistonji will complete all legal formalities,' says Miraben, and then adds, sensing a touch of discontent, 'Neelima, are you fine with this?'

'Yes, ma,' says Neelima and starts to cry. The last month has been traumatic for her in more ways than anyone could imagine. Neelima was the closest to her brother Mihir, and only Mihir knew how close she was to Rajiv Mehra. Or so she thinks. The call record findings made by the police, and since disclosed to Rupesh, have been duly conveyed to Miraben.

'Let us put the tragedy in the past,' says Miraben. 'Mihir would have wanted that. Let us—' and here Miraben eyes Neelima '—let us choose our friends wisely and our relationships sensibly.'

After dinner, as Neelima is being driven home, she scrolls through the photos in her phone, of Mihir, of Rajiv, of Rajiv and Neelima, together in happier times.

A teardrop spatters on a photo of a smiling Rajiv, blurring it.

* * *

Inspector Apte rubs his eyes and extends his hand for the coffee cup. It is approaching midnight. He has been staring at the desktop screen for a little more than six hours, screening the Taaj CCTV footage. He has been the only one in the research wing for three hours now; except of course for the duty-bound Raut keeping a vigil just outside, on call to cater to his superior's every need. Raut has placed Nair's desk bell on Inspector Apte's table. It has been rung three times—once for coffee, the second time for dinner—a vada-pav take-out— and the third for a notepad. Raut's head is lolling, and he is moments away from falling asleep. But he dare not. The bell can ring any moment, and ignoring it could mean a dressing-down from his boss Nair.

Meanwhile inside, Apte, getting restless himself, fast-forwards the footage as much as he can afford to. He has seen those parts of the footage that were shown in the court multiple times; he found nothing new or out of the ordinary there. He makes a note of the exact time Rajiv Mehra and Emanuele are engrossed in a conversation and then disappear into a chamber. The time stamp shows 6.45 p.m. There is no footage of what transpired inside the chamber, only when they both emerge from it, at 7.15 p.m., and resume their respective tasks. The next duration of interest—again, this was shown as evidence in the court—is when the CCTV captures Rajiv preparing the soufflé. The dessert plates are arranged in neat rows and columns, and they are all monogrammed with the initials of the guests. Rajiv takes out a bottle and, at 7.27 p.m., carefully mixes its contents with the base of the soufflé, but only for the plate monogrammed with—as Inspector Apte had informed the court—the initials of Mihir Kothari. This was, Apte had told the judge, to ensure the cyanide-laced soufflé could only be consumed by the person Rajiv intended to murder.

Nothing much to decipher or any new angle to discover emerges as the footage plays on. Inspector Apte is getting exasperated and restless. He yawns extendedly and stretches his arms, and then rewinds, to screen the morning's footage. He sees Rajiv Mehra arriving at the hotel; he sees, from a different CCTV camera on the panel, Rajiv being escorted to his suite, at 11.35 a.m., and then him exiting it along with the hotel manager at 11.41 a.m.

Inspector Apte decides to focus only on this particular CCTV camera, which captures the corridor leading to Rajiv's suite. This was not shown in the court as there was no need felt for it. The tape runs for an extended period; housekeeping staff and other guests are seen entering and leaving the corridor—Apte fast-forwards the clip and then plays it at normal speed whenever people appear on the screen. At 7.01 p.m., there is movement in the corridor. A man, with only his back visible, is pushing the housekeeping trolley away from the camera and along the corridor. Apte perks up and straightens his back. The man brings the trolley to a halt in front of the Maharaja suite, swipes the card, and enters. There is no one else in the corridor. Seconds pass, turning to minutes. Apte's eyes are glued to the screen. Then, seven minutes later, at 7.08 p.m., Rajiv Mehra exits his suite. He walks towards the camera and reaches the lift lobby, pressing the escalator button. The lift door slides open and he steps in.

Apte pauses the tape. He selects the camera placed inside the lift and plays the tape, moving the bar swiftly to 7.08 p.m. There is Rajiv, inside the lift.

Apte notes down the time. His hand is trembling. Sweat beads have appeared on his forehead. He switches to the earlier CCTV panel, the one that showed Rajiv and Emanuele in an animated conversation. Rajiv and Emanuele exit the chamber next to the kitchen at 7.15 p.m. and leave each other's company to go about their business. At 7.27 p.m., Rajiv mixes the cyanide in the soufflé dessert bowl.

Inspector Apte has at long last begun to link the jigsaw pieces. He shuffles on his seat and goes back to the Maharaja suite corridor footage, playing it for the next few hours, fast-forwarding it when there is no movement or activity. At 10.09 p.m., Rajiv appears in the corridor. With him are Inspector Apte and his two colleagues. They walk along the corridor and enter the Maharaja suite. At 10.25 p.m., the ambulance attendants emerge from the lift along with a stretcher that they wheel to the Maharaja suite. At 10.30 p.m., Rajiv emerges from the suite on the stretcher, along with Apte and the others. Inspector Apte jerks back on his chair and scribbles the timings on the pad. Rajiv first entered the suite at 11.35 a.m., and then exited the suite at 11.41 a.m. and then again at 7.08 p.m. The pencil drops from Inspector Apte's hand. He wipes his brow and flicks the sweat away. '*Bhen chod*,' he says, exhaling the invective slowly. How can Rajiv enter his suite only once but exit twice?

A chill runs down Inspector Apte's spine. 'This cannot be true. My eyes are deceiving me,' he says to himself, gulping down the rest of the coffee in one go. He rubs his eyes and steams his glasses and wipes them with his shirt cuff and starts all over again, this time going carefully and methodically over the entire day's footage. He knows the drill by heart now. His quivering fingers click at the CCTV panels as they shuffle and come together as pieces of a puzzle. The story is shaping up in his head.

It takes him another hour to complete it. His eyes are bloodshot, and his mouth is dry. He arches his back and the pencil slides from his hand. It is indeed true. Rajiv entered his room once but exited twice. It is absurd, unbelievable. He cannot comprehend how this could happen. Was there another passageway to the Maharaja suite that is not visible on the CCTV? Impossible. Did Rajiv enter his room through a window or a fire escape? Impossible again. He has been in the suite, and he remembers distinctly that it had no other doors or entrances or exits except the one that opens into the corridor covered by the CCTV.

He goes back to the CCTV panel of that evening's recording, 7.08 p.m. to be precise. He zooms into Rajiv's face as he emerges from his suite. It is indeed Rajiv. There is no doubt about it. He opens the window of the CCTV screenshot of Rajiv exiting at 11.41 a.m. and places them side-by-side. Both are Rajiv, identical in every respect. Apte throws the pencil and the pad away in frustration. He cannot solve this; and he knows it. He also knows that Rajiv is dead. A feeling of immense futility overcomes him. *What is the use of this; why am I pursuing it?* But then he remembers Gurmukh and the lie. Something is not right about this case. He must rethink it carefully if he has to make some sense of this. It may all lead to a wild goose chase, but then Inspector Apte is not one to leave a loose end untied. Besides, it is not as if he is pressed for time and preoccupied with work these days. This is a welcome change. That's right, he says to himself, 'I have experienced more excitement and thrill in the last six hours than I have in the last six weeks.' He gets up from the chair, collects his notes, ejects the security footage CD, drops it into his bag and marches out, acknowledging the salute from the surprised and flustered Raut, who barely manages to murmur a request for signing the register. 'Tell Nair I am taking the CD and will return it tomorrow after making a copy,' says Apte without looking back.

'Rajiv walks in once, he walks out twice,' mutters Inspector Apte inside the elevator, and then inside his car and then all the way home. *Rajiv walks in once, he walks out twice.*

* * *

6

Rajiv peels away from the tourist group and wanders inside the Satua Baba Ashram. The open courtyard is like an oasis in the middle of the bustling city. It's as though its noises have been sucked away by a vacuum cleaner. A giant banyan tree stands in the centre, and its canopy extends to all corners of the courtyard, with some branches having taken root on the first floor of the row of rooms that run all around the rectangular two-storey structure.

Rajiv goes and sits on the chabutra under the banyan tree. He picks up the ladle placed on top of an earthen pot and scoops out some water to splash his face with. No one disturbs him. A few sadhus are strolling about. On closer inspection Rajiv realizes that they are all foreigners. He proceeds to the ashram reception.

'Namaste,' says Rajiv to the receptionist, a man in his thirties with a shaven head except for a tuft at the back.

The man greets Rajiv warmly. 'How can I help you?' he asks.

'I'd like to stay in the ashram,' says Rajiv. 'But I have no money.'

'That's not an issue. All guests help out in any way they can. Can you teach young children? Can you cook?'

'Yes.'

'This is your home, then. We also pay a token amount to ashramites who help or contribute in any way in our activities.'

'Thank you.'

'You are welcome. You can sleep in the dorm. I'll send someone to show you around our kitchen and the school. We have a few rules. No mobile phones. You can come here and make a call—STD or ISD—anytime of the day you want. And we provide to every guest our own ashram clothing.'

'That's fine by me.'

'Great. Welcome to the ashram. Mohan ji here will take you to the dorm,' says the receptionist, handing Rajiv a set of clean dhoti and kurta. Rajiv nods at Mohan ji and together they make their way across the courtyard to the dormitory from where Rajiv will begin a new chapter in his life.

* * *

The mood is sombre. The courtyard is packed with mourners dressed in white. It is the *tehrawin* rite of Inspector Sharad Munde. His giant garlanded photo leans on the table and watches over the proceedings. Police officers walk up to the platform where Munde's widow is seated to pay their respects and comfort her. Inspector Apte is in the line too, right behind Inspector Ganesh. Apte crouches down and consoles Mrs Munde. He speaks to her of the honesty and sacrifice of his departed colleague. He must have tried to free himself and others in the Scorpio, he tells her softly. Never met a braver officer; it is a loss for the entire police force and a personal one for me as I knew him well. Mrs Munde sniffles and dabs her nose with her pallu. Apte steps aside to let others pay their respects.

The gathering thins. Apte and Ganesh step outside the courtyard, Ganesh narrating to Apte the entire incident and what transpired afterwards, starting with the accident on the Sion highway. All five stood no chance, he says.

Apte nods. 'You inspected the Scorpio that was fished out?'

'Yes,' says Ganesh. 'It was a mangled piece of steel, almost beyond recognition. It must have hit a rock at the bottom of the river. The windshield and window were cracked to pieces. Terrible way to go.'

'Yes,' agrees Apte. There is silence while both reflect on the tragedy. Apte switches lanes. 'So. How's the commissioner treating you guys? Was all his anger reserved for only me?'

Ganesh smirks. 'Sir, you don't know the half of it. It has gotten worse. You know how it is. The coterie decides, and it comes down on us to do the dirty work. Nothing has changed. In fact, I'd say you were lucky to have escaped the worst.'

'Ha, yes, mock me Ganesh, go on,' taunts Apte.

'I'm serious, sir. Take this case itself,' says Ganesh.

Apte's ears perk up. 'What do you mean?' he asks. 'I thought the case was closed after all five bodies were found and identified?'

'Yes,' says Ganesh, then lowers his voice. 'Officially closed.'

'Go on,' prods Apte, interested.

Ganesh clears his throat and says conspiratorially, 'Five bodies were arranged on the floor, wrapped in white sheets. The press came and took photos. They were handed a communiqué stating that DNA testing identified the bodies to be of four policemen and Rajiv Mehra. What they don't know, what no one knows, is that only four bodies were recovered from the Scorpio. Rajiv's body was never found.'

Apte is stunned. He doesn't know how to react. Words fail him. He shakes his head. 'What do you mean, Ganesh? Be clear.'

'I am being clear, sir,' insists Ganesh. 'I'm telling you this because you were in charge of the case. In fact, had you not superannuated, landing the whole responsibility on my shoulders, the commissioner would have ordered you to do what he asked me to—add another body to the four and make it look like it was Rajiv's.'

A chill runs down Apte's spine. 'But how is this possible? Have you gone mad, Ganesh? Why, where was the need?' he asks indignantly.

'Who knows, sir,' replies Ganesh calmly. 'It never comes down to us, does it? We don't decide the need. We just make it happen. And I made it happen—I transported a body from the King George's Hospital morgue in the middle of the night and disfigured it, then added Rajiv's DNA report to those of the four policemen, our Munde being one of them. No one knows this except the commissioner and I and Bhogle, who helped me with the dead body and the DNA report. And now you.'

'But this is crazy,' frowns Apte. His mind is awash with scenarios and their consequences. He doesn't even want to contemplate what this can mean, when one adds to it his findings from the CCTV footage. He steadies himself. 'So, what you are saying, Ganesh, is that Rajiv might be alive?'

Ganesh shakes his head. 'No chance of that, sir. To be fair to commissioner sahab, he wanted the case closed to protect himself and the department from all the hounding and the terrible press we were getting. I'll be frank with you. Even I think Rajiv is dead. No one could have escaped from that Scorpio alive. Impossible. Trust me. And even if one in a million chance that someone did, just two hundred yards downstream is the waterfall and then a deep river below, full of sharp rocks. It is my belief that Rajiv, although he managed to extricate himself from the Scorpio, was killed soon after and his body, if it reached ashore, was eaten by animals.'

'Sure. My belief. Exactly what is prescribed in the police manual. Rajiv could be alive. He could be out of the country by now, living a good life. In fact, an even better life, now that he knows the case has been closed.'

'But, sir—'

Apte is livid and for the first time in a very long time he cannot hide it. 'This was my case, damn it. I worked my ass off for it, ensured watertight evidence, obtained a conviction, and then, unknown to me, the main accused is missing, not presumed dead but shown dead, just because the commissioner or his handler up the chain decides the case needs to be closed. This is bullshit, Ganesh.'

Ganesh tries to mollify Apte. 'I know what you mean, sir, but trust me. Had you seen the wreckage and the accident spot and the whole scene, you would have said the same thing I am saying now. In fact, I don't think Rajiv escaped from the Scorpio at all. I think he died in there along with the others and then in the ensuing days his body freed itself from the cabin and floated out and went downstream.'

'Sure. Only his body. Not the others,' hisses Apte.

'It can happen, sir,' says Ganesh.

There is silence. A whole minute passes. Apte nods and looks at Ganesh and sneers. 'Case closed.'

'Case closed,' reddens Ganesh, evading Apte's eyes. He shakes Apte's hand and walks away, promising to meet up for a drink soon.

Apte wanders slowly to his car and climbs inside. He puts on the seatbelt and turns on the ignition. And then he exhales a sigh. Rajiv might not be dead. And he might not have killed Mihir.

What am I to do? asks Apte of himself, tapping the steering wheel as the car idles. He knows exactly what. He needs to speak to Emanuele and for that, he needs access to his case notes and papers—being nibbled on by rats right now in the Mumbai Police HQ store. He puts the car into gear and drives away in a hurry, leaving behind a swirling cloud of dust.

* * *

He is inside the air-conditioning duct, crawling on his knees and elbows, cursing after every forward movement. The stink is overpowering. The duct hasn't been cleaned for years. He clicks on his mobile phone and consults the ammonia print map of the Mumbai Police HQ seventh floor, in particular the area where the evidence and research room is situated. He revisits the sketch he had drawn of the room when he was there two nights ago. Another hundred odd yards to go. He swears and commences his crawl. Rats scuttle alongside him, making a clanking, echoing noise as though someone is tapping a metal sheet with a stick. He tears through cobwebs that resemble a lace sheer, slithers over pools of water with scum and algae floating on them, curses to no end, but never loses focus.

He checks his Rolex. It is approaching 1 a.m. The new duty constable will be taking over the research room watch just about now. He better hurry along.

At long last, he arrives at the end of the air duct. Under him is the louvred vent. It is pitch dark inside the research room. He unscrews the vent carefully and jumps down, making no sound. He tiptoes to where the CCTV footage CDs are stacked. The phone torch is too bright, so he gets to work using only the screen light. His fingers gallop over the CD collection, hunting out the date he is looking for. Suddenly the lights outside the room come on. Abandoning his search, he scrambles to the floor. The door swings open. The research wing is illuminated with a plank of light coming from the offices outside. A silhouette stands on the threshold, immobile, listening for any movement, and when satisfied, retreats, closing the door.

He breathes a sigh and switches on his phone screen and gets to work again. He finds the month and the week. But the Taaj footage CD is missing. He checks the entire stack again, in case someone slotted it wrongly. But it isn't there. He checks the other stacks. The Taaj CD is not in those stacks, either. For the first time, he finds that he is sweating.

The conclusion is clear. Someone else is hunting for the same thing that he is. The chase is on. He climbs into the duct and commences the painful journey back, carefully bolting the vent behind him.

* * *

It is just after lunch. Inspector Apte is in his office. He has the papers and his notes from the Kothari murder case spread in front of him. He dials Emanuele's home. A woman answers after a few rings. Apte clears his throat. 'Buon giorno,' he says, having practised the greeting beforehand, 'I am calling from India. May I speak with Mr Emanuele Tardelli?'

'Who is this?' asks the woman.

'Are you Mrs Tardelli?' asks Apte.

'Si, si,' comes the reply.

'Madam, I am Inspector Apte, from the Mumbai Police. I would like to talk with Mr Emanuele Tardelli. Is he at home?'

There is a pause at the other end. Inspector Apte waits expectantly. He hears a sniffle. 'Hello?' he prods.

'Emanuele is no more. He died two weeks ago,' says the woman, sobbing.

'Oh. I am so sorry, madam,' says Apte, shocked. He collects himself quickly. 'How did he . . . ?'

'Heart attack. He had gone fishing,' replies the woman.

'I am very sorry, Mrs Tardelli. My apologies for disturbing you,' says Apte and bids a polite goodbye. He places the receiver on the hook slowly, taking the news in. The last man who talked to Rajiv is dead. He stares at the abstract painting in front, mulling his options.

* * *

Dressed in a breezy floral halter neck Versace creation, a mother of pearl necklace accentuating her collarbones, art deco sunglasses concealing her eyes, Louboutins embellishing her feet, a lacquer chopstick spearing her casually knotted bun, Neelima Kothari Thapar is beauty and splendour personified.

She is at the Shamiana, Taaj, for a laid-back brunch with her husband, Krishan Thapar.

Paired with him, one gets the doomed impression that she is a trophy, for Krishan is a brusque, ill-mannered, balding, overweight man, a hackneyed small-town businessman turned defence dealer tycoon. His lumpy upper body is squeezed into a tight polo and stone rings glint on every one of his eight beefy fingers as he chomps on his cigar and gestures rudely with his forefinger every other minute for attention. The waiters swarm round him, but he makes them wait uncomfortably to catch what they have been summoned to the table for. Neelima is mortified and embarrassed, and thankful that she is wearing dark glasses. They haven't conversed since they took the table. Krishan has continually been on his Vertu phone.

Neelima wishes she were elsewhere. In fact, she is. In her mind, she is rereading the pages of her bedside novel. She has developed this habit lately; it allows her to withstand the company of her husband. She is forced to break away from her rumination by the sight of an approaching armada of waiters, led by the Michelin-star chef Rajiv Mehra. The lunch has arrived.

The waiters place the dishes on the tray table and await further instructions. Rajiv greets the Thapars warmly—only Neelima acknowledges him; Krishan is still on the phone—and gets ready to serve them, beginning with Neelima. He explains the dish, its origin and ingredients, but is interrupted midway by Krishan, who covers the phone with his palm and informs Neelima he has to leave for an important client meeting. He doesn't apologize, simply pushes back his chair and trudges off. Rajiv is miffed, but he hides it. Neelima glances up. Rajiv realizes she is looking at him through the dark glasses. He smiles. 'That's a lot of food for one person.'

Neelima stretches her lips reluctantly to fashion a smile. 'Would you like to join me, chef?'

Rajiv is startled by the offer. He grins sheepishly, not knowing what to say.

'Oh, come on,' says Neelima, 'Don't be a bore. Besides, this way if the grub is awful, it's only fair the one who cooked it should get to eat it, too.'

Rajiv chuckles. He pulls up ae chair and sits down. 'Thank you,' he says, removing his hat and apron.

Neelima is struck by how handsome he is. She toys with her necklace. 'What would you like, red or white, or some champagne?' she asks.

Rajiv opts for the white. 'It goes well with the starters,' he says. They begin their lunch. The conversation starts to flow freely, and Neelima is thankful for the company. They talk about food, about travel, about corporate culture and art. They laugh and smile and make jokes. Rajiv tells her of his struggles. Neelima tells him she has never had to struggle. An hour passes. It feels as though they have known each other for years. Neelima hasn't been this happy in months.

'What are your plans after lunch?' she asks.

'Back to the frying pan,' says Rajiv.

'You never take a break?'

'Need to make preparations for the evening event,' sighs Rajiv.

'Ah.'

'The chief minister will be dining here tonight.'

'He doesn't deserve you and your masterpieces.'

'Anyone who can pay for them deserves my masterpieces.'

'Even corrupt politicians and underworld dons?'

'Why, don't they have to eat? Their beating hearts are not corrupt or criminal, are they?'

'Every beating heart is corrupt *and* criminal.'

'You are right there,' smiles Rajiv.

'Tell me, would you gift a Picasso to a blind man?'

Rajiv is fascinated and taken aback by the question, the sharpness with which it is asked. He searches for an answer. Neelima senses it.

'Take it easy, chef,' she comforts. 'I didn't mean to be rude. Of course, everyone has a right to your masterpieces. All I am saying is, not everyone can appreciate them.'

'Maybe. As I said, anyone who can pay for them deserves them.'

'And what about your time? Can anyone who can pay for it get it?'

'Depends.'

'That's hypocrisy right there,' smiles Neelima.

'Why so?'

'You spend your precious time creating your masterpieces. And as you said, anyone who can pay for them can have them. Essentially, they are paying for your time.'

This is new for Rajiv, and exhilarating. Not often, in fact rarely if ever, does he find himself challenged with such dazzling retorts. 'So what you are proposing,' he says, 'is that instead of serving masterpieces, I should instead serve my time on a platter. That it's one and the same thing?'

'Bravo,' smiles Neelima. 'You're getting there, chef. Let me rephrase. What would Picasso prefer—to sell his masterpiece to a blind man, or to offer the blind man the length of time he has taken to make that masterpiece?'

'That's deep,' admits Rajiv. 'But let me turn it around. What would the blind man prefer—to own Picasso's masterpiece, or to be in the company of Picasso for the length of time Picasso has taken to make that masterpiece?'

'If I was the blind man, the latter.'

'Even though it would be fleeting? While the masterpiece would be with the blind man forever?'

'But what would the blind man do with the masterpiece? He cannot see it. He cannot sense the brilliance, the beauty, the plan, the effort, the idea, the genius.'

Rajiv knows he has been beaten. He raises his glass. 'Here's to you—blind man or Picasso?'

'Blind man,' grins Neelima. 'And I want Picasso's time.'

'That's cheating. You have already tasted his masterpiece.'

Now it is Neelima's turn to be tongue-tied. But she recovers quickly. 'See,' she counters. 'I had your masterpiece. It's gone—the pleasure was momentary. It's no longer there with me. Just like the blind man cannot value the masterpiece even though he owns it.'

'That's not entirely true, is it though,' says Rajiv. 'Don't you have memories of the masterpiece you owned, even though fleetingly? Recall them and feel happy again.'

'Yes, but can remembrances give me the same happiness as the real thing? Can I enliven my senses with them? Can I taste my memories? They are a poor substitute.'

'I agree. So, you'd like Picasso's time instead, then, I take it,' jokes Rajiv.

'Any day. I am asking you the price. Of your time. Right now.'

Rajiv is dying to lower Neelima's shades.

'Answer, Picasso,' she says.

'It's free.'

She throws her head back and laughs. Getting up, she grabs Rajiv's hand. 'C'mon then, Picasso. I have you for the next few hours.'

Rajiv smiles, standing too. 'Do you always win?' he asks. 'Why do I get the feeling this was a trap from the beginning?'

Neelima turns around and tilts her head playfully. 'Well, taming Picasso is never easy, is it. Hurry up, Pablo. Tick-tock, tick-tock. We haven't got all day.'

And it is then, with Neelima dragging him by his wrist and him trying to avoid crashing into tables and other guests, that Rajiv notices her prosthetic leg.

They are at the Gateway of India. Neelima hasn't let go of Rajiv's wrist. People are staring at them.

'What do you want to do?' she asks.

'You tell me. You are the one who has bought my time.'

Neelima smiles mischievously. 'Let's go to Elephanta.'

Rajiv nods, now increasingly conscious of the stares all around. He lets his hand go limp so Neelima will release his wrist. But she doesn't. They descend the embankment steps—coarse granite smoothened by a century of seawater and grime, as slippery as temple flooring. 'Careful!' shouts Rajiv. But Neelima is in no mood to listen. She reminds Rajiv of Waheeda Rehman's screw-the-world solo act in *aaj phir jeene ki tammana hai* in *Guide*—all that pent-up energy and then its unintended release. He shakes his head and laughs.

'I thought you would have your own yacht docked here somewhere,' quips Rajiv as they climb aboard a ferry.

'I do, as a matter of fact,' says Neelima. 'But the ride might be more enjoyable on this one.'

A sizeable crowd has trooped aboard and soon the ferry is crammed. Neelima and Rajiv move to the upper deck. The breeze is liberating. The sun has gone behind a cloud, and it looks as though it might rain. They lean their elbows on the railing and gaze out. Down below in the waters, urchins bob up and down, imploring them to throw in coins. The newly married couple standing next to Neelima is intrigued. Egged on by the wife, the man tosses a coin. As it lands in the choppy water and disappears, one among the boys flips a somersault and dives. He emerges a few seconds later, holding aloft the coin in his hand. And as is the rule, he keeps it. Neelima shakes Rajiv's arm, beseeching him. Rajiv fishes out a coin from his hip pocket and throws it in the water. Two boys race and dive for it. One of them emerges with the coin. Neelima applauds.

'Wouldn't it be better to just give the money to them?' Rajiv ponders out loud.

'But that would be begging. Here they have earned it,' says Neelima.

'I must admit it is sad to watch this.'

'Why? People earn. They work for their money. Are you sad to watch people work for their money?'

'I am talking of just these kids.'

'I see no difference. They are happy. They are working. They are earning their money.'

'But they struggle for something that you'd have given them happily, or you could afford to give them happily. What do you prefer: that money comes to you on its own, or that you have to put your life in danger for it? Be honest.'

Neelima looks into the distance. 'The myth of Sisyphus,' she whispers to herself.

Rajiv hears it. 'The what of what?'

Neelima smiles. 'There is only one really serious philosophical problem remaining, and that is suicide.'

Rajiv takes it in. Silence ensues.

'Camus wrote that,' says Neelima. 'He wondered why would a man, Sisyphus, roll a rock every single day of his life up a hill, only to release it and watch it roll back down, and then roll it up again. Why? Why doesn't he just commit suicide, instead? That's the absurdity of life. It is purposeless; it is futile. You can see your future. You can see your death. It is inevitable. And yet you don't commit suicide. You want to live, despite pain and sorrow and agony and ugliness. Why?'

'Yes, why?'

'Because the struggle alone is enough to fill a man's heart, and one must imagine Sisyphus to be happy.'

Rajiv wants to hold Neelima's hand but resists. 'You are saying you can lose everything and yet be the same person because you know the end?'

'In a way, yes.'

Rajiv is about to go against his better judgment. He knows it. But something, he knows not what, makes him do it. He snatches Neelima's Fendi handbag from her arm and empties it over the railing, shaking it until all its contents— currency, cards, coins, lipsticks, glasses, wallet, mobile phone, tumble down and plop into the sea below. The boys go mad, scampering and diving. The waters froth with all the thrashing. Then, one by one, they come up for air, holding the contents. One boy has the phone, another the wallet, the third the glasses. And all through this mayhem, this mad scramble, Neelima's expression hasn't altered. Not a muscle has twitched. 'It's theirs now,' she says with a smile.

Rajiv is stunned. He is racked with guilt. He wants to apologize. But instead, something, possibly the truth-or-dare quirk in Neelima, pushes him to up the ante. 'All these things, the contents of your bag,' he gesticulates, 'weren't important to you. Maybe that's why you didn't care. But what if you were to throw away something that's vital to you, a part of you . . .'

Even before Rajiv can finish the sentence, Neelima lifts her dress to above her knee and unbuckles her prosthetic leg and tosses it overboard with trademark impassiveness.

Rajiv staggers back, flabbergasted. Without a second's thought he steps on to the railing and jumps into the water. The prosthetic leg jounces as though it has a life of its own and descends with speed, but Rajiv is right behind, and he grabs it just as it is about to hit the ocean floor. He buckles his knees and shoots up and a few seconds later emerges above the surface. The urchins clap and hoot while the crowd on the ferry is too stunned to react. Rajiv wipes his face with his palm as he bobs in the water. He looks up. Neelima is waving at him. He knows that he will remember her expression till his dying day. It is love.

The ferry is finally on its way to the Elephanta caves. Rajiv is standing next to Neelima, his hands grasping the railing. His shirt and his trousers are dripping, and he is drenched to the bone. 'Neelima,' he murmurs. She turns her head slowly, as though lost in thought. The breeze has driven back her tresses.

'I don't know what to say, Neelima.'

'Say nothing. Just be with me. Be in this moment. Nothing matters; nothing at all.'

They spend the next few hours strolling around the Elephanta caves. They talk continually; tell each other

everything there is to tell, about their present and past lives.
They laugh, they turn serious, they feel like crying, they mock
each other, crack jokes, they hug, embrace, walk hand in hand.
They kiss. As they separate, Rajiv looks into Neelima's eyes.
'Can I ask you something?'

She nods.

'All through our lunch, our stroll, the ferry trip, our time
here, you haven't removed your shades. You have looked into
my heart and I into yours, but you haven't allowed me to look
into your eyes.'

Neelima doesn't respond.

'Can I?' says Rajiv, and without waiting for a response
or allowing Neelima enough time to react, removes her dark
glasses.

Neelima has a black eye. Her left brow has stitches.

The shades fall from Rajiv's grasp. Anger rises in him. He
knows who did it. 'I'm sorry,' he says.

'Don't be,' says Neelima. 'Now you know why I didn't
remove the shades.'

Rajiv ponders over it. 'I actually don't,' he says. 'You are
the same person who didn't flinch a muscle when I tossed the
contents of your handbag into the sea. You didn't even let me
finish my sentence before you threw away your precious leg.
But here—this . . . no. I don't understand.'

'Rajiv Mehra,' says Neelima, her eyes an ocean of sadness
and yet sparkling, 'Whatever your feelings have been for me
these past few hours, they have been a reaction to who I am,
my mind, my thoughts. You kissed me because you wanted
to. You walked with me because you wanted to. I didn't force
you into anything. Your feelings came naturally to you. They
were pure. But had you seen me without my shades, you'd

have imagined me differently. Your feelings would have been tinged with remorse, pity for me; you'd have slotted me as a victim, of domestic violence, of misfortune, wanting compassion, empathy. You'd have thought of me as yearning for your company as a means of escape. I saved you from that pretence.'

The setting sun blazes across the horizon. Neelima's face is radiant. Rajiv holds it in his palms. 'I love you,' he whispers. He kisses her again. They walk back to the ferry holding hands.

The trip back is made in beautiful, comforting silence. As they alight at the Gateway, Rajiv asks for her number.

Neelima smiles. 'First you throw away my phone and now you ask me for my number.'

They laugh their hearts out. 'Let's take a selfie then, at least,' appeals Rajiv. Neelima agrees. Rajiv takes out his phone and they click a selfie. 'I'll WhatsApp it to you. Once I have your number,' he says as they part ways.

Lying on her bed in her home, that selfie is what Neelima is gazing at. She thinks of Rajiv, and of what Camus said, and suddenly everything fits. There is but one serious philosophical problem, and that is suicide.

* * *

7

It is drizzling. Rajiv has had his evening meal and is negotiating the thick crowds on the streets of Varanasi, unmindful of the hustle and bustle and the cacophony. Hawkers approach him, so do beggars, and some among the general public, to take his blessings, but he looks into the distance and walks past without even so much as acknowledging them; they don't exist for him—how can they if he doesn't exist in the first place? Everything is maya, a figment of Mahakaal's imagination, and he alone will decide when to destroy it.

The twilight has given way to nightfall, and the wet roads shimmer as yellow light from the streetlamps falls on them. Rajiv turns a corner and abruptly the noise and the crowds vanish. He is by himself. The area is new to him, and he doesn't recognize it. He pauses and looks around, and then resumes his walk. Turning another corner, he realizes he is being followed. He enters a congested lane and breaks into a run. Long, stretching shadows form on the loose-brick houses that line the street, one of Rajiv and the other of the man chasing him. Rajiv slows down as he comes to a dead end.

A mound of excavated earth blocks the lane; cement water pipes are strewn around it, hedged in by a wire mesh fence. He clambers over it frantically and manages to drop down to the other side. He starts to run again. He does not know where the winding street is taking him or who is following him, but he doesn't look back.

He finally comes to a halt outside a desolate temple. Hands on knees, he takes a breather. A loud thunderclap shakes Rajiv out of his stupor; the bolt of lightning that follows in its wake illuminates the sky and he looks up. Grey ominous clouds are hanging low and may burst at any moment. He struggles over to the hand pump by the temple and goes down on his haunches, placing his open mouth under the spout and guzzling down water even as he operates the pump with one hand. Having had his fill, he straightens, and as he does, he is grabbed by the neck. He fights to wrench himself away. He flails his arms and tries to shake off the man, but it is hopeless.

'Who are you?' he cries. There is no response. The crook of the attacker's arm squeezes in. Rajiv is about to lose consciousness. He bites the arm as a last-ditch attempt. The arm relaxes its grip and in that split second Rajiv manages to extricate himself. He starts to run again, except that now he is being chased not only by his attacker but also by a pack of ferocious dogs. They are howling and barking and hounding him. Rajiv cannot keep up. He collapses on the road. The dogs close in on him, growling menacingly, ready to rip him to shreds.

The man appears, and the dogs move back and spread out as though they are under his control. He bends down and grabs Rajiv's wrists and starts to drag him. The tarmac scrapes his back and legs, bloodying them. Rajiv is in excruciating pain.

He cries for help, but no one hears him. There is no escape. The dogs scamper all around Rajiv's body as it is hauled through the streets, all the way to the Manikarnika Ghat. There are people waiting there for him, but Rajiv cannot see their faces. It is too dark. The man stops and releases his grip on Rajiv's wrists. A hush descends. Even the dogs go quiet. The only sound filtering through to the ghat is from across the Ganga. It is the whistling wind, steadily increasing in intensity.

The man lifts Rajiv clean-off the earth and deposits him on top of a ready pyre. Rajiv resists; he wants to get up and jump off, but he has no strength left; the only muscles working in his body are of his face, and they shape up to show fear. The man retreats and so does the pack of dogs. A pundit approaches the pyre. He is bare-chested with a knotted tuft of hair at the back of his head. A *janehu* runs diagonally across his torso. He steps on to the platform. Rajiv cannot see his face, only watch him circling the pyre with an earthen pot on his shoulder, chanting Vedic verses. The pot has a hole near the bottom through which water is pouring out. After seven rounds, the pundit stops and allows the pot to fall over his shoulder. It crashes to the ground and breaks into a hundred pieces. The man who dragged Rajiv through the streets steps out from the circle of people around the pyre and hands the pundit a burning torch. The pundit holds it aloft and glares at Rajiv and then traces the torch all around the pyre. The timber catches fire and crackles, expelling a spray of embers. Rajiv shrieks, but no one comes to help him. The pyre is now engulfed in flames that lick at the wood.

Rajiv knows this is his end. He closes his eyes and is transported to a villa in Tuscany. It belongs to his friend, the blind opera tenor Andrea Bocelli. It is his birthday and Rajiv, along with Emanuele, has prepared a sumptuous family feast. Andrea's home is alive with the merry sounds of children playing in the lawns and friends laughing and chatting around a crackling bonfire. Rajiv recollects the beauty of the villa. It was magnificent, and curated exquisitely, with every item chosen personally by Bocelli. And then, lying on the pyre, about to die, Rajiv realizes that Bocelli, blind by birth, can never see the beauty of his house, only imagine it. And if Bocelli can only imagine beauty, why does his house have to be beautiful in reality? It could be a dilapidated, crumbling, damp ruin. So is beauty real or imagined? Does it lie in the eye of the beholder or in his mind? And if it doesn't have to be real for someone to derive pleasure out of it, isn't pleasure imagined as well? And it follows that if pleasure is imagined, everything else is, including grief and sorrow and pain and death. Rajiv is heaving the last of his breaths. He can feel the fire lick at his legs. It won't be long now.

He opens his eyes for one last time. And now he can see the faces of the men and women standing around him, staring at him. There is Subhadra and the Taaj manager and the crown prince, and Rupesh and Neelima and Emanuele and Inspector Apte and the judge. Rajiv screams and swings his head from side to side, but he does not have the strength to get up. His muscles and his will slacken at last; life is about to leave his body. His head falls to one side. And then he sees the face of the pundit. It is Mihir. Rajiv grits his teeth and opens his mouth to exhale one last time. Just at that instant, the waters of the Ganga begin to rumble and roll. It is as though the energy of their every atom has amalgamated into one entity. Boats are tossed around like matchsticks, the waters froth and growl as the wind tears through them. The spectacle is mesmerizing. Rajiv, his body on fire, cranes his neck to have a look. A great wave has formed, and it is approaching the Manikarnika Ghat at immense speed. Rajiv closes his eyes and waits for the moment. It arrives. The wave crashes into the ghat with the sound of a nuclear explosion and consumes the pyre and everyone around it. The land and everything on it go under water. Rajiv is descending, the burning logs of the pyre cartwheeling all around him. Dead bodies are everywhere; they collide with Rajiv as he descends into the abyss. He flaps his arms and thrashes his legs and tries to swim up, but he can't. His body is spinning as it descends. Soon he reaches the riverbed. He sees a gun and picks it up and fires and keeps firing until he hears the empty clicks of the revolver. But it is futile. Bubbles escape from his mouth and the last one seeps out with a colossal sucking sound. This is the end.

Rajiv shoots up from his bed, heaving and panting. Sweat is pouring down his face and neck. He is too dazed to react. He looks around, his gasping having subsided a little. His fellow ashramites snore on adjacent beds without a care in the world. Rajiv drags himself to the water cooler and glugs down a jug of water. He pours some water in the hollow of his palm and hits his face with it. The nightmares don't seem to end. The tranquillity he yearned for and thought would come to him in the ashram hasn't materialized. Something is amiss. He has to do something. He has to act. He thought being dead to the world would allow him to live the life he had always wanted. But now he realizes that his new life was an imagined one. It could not be made real. He was blinded by his vision.

Rajiv struggles back to his bed and collapses, his eyes wide open. 'I am not blind,' he says to himself. 'I need to reclaim my reality, my past and my present, not imagine my future.' He looks up at the wall clock. It is a quarter past midnight. There is a faint light coming from the reception. Rajiv gets up and walks towards it. The man at the desk is the security guard. He is fast asleep. Rajiv shakes his shoulder gently. He opens his eyes with a start.

'I want to make an international call,' says Rajiv. 'You can put it on my account.'

'The phone is not working. Go back to sleep,' replies the man in a miffed tone.

Rajiv takes out a hundred-rupee note and slips it in the man's pocket. Without waiting for a reaction, he pulls the phone towards him and dials a number. A female voice answers from the other end.

'Is that Maria?' asks Rajiv.

'Yes,' says the woman intrigued. 'Who is this?'

'Is Emanuele there? It must be, what, eight at your end? Or is he at the restaurant?' asks Rajiv.

'Who is this?' repeats the woman.

'I am Emanuele's Indian friend. We've never met, Maria, but I know so much about you. Emanuele talks about you all the time. Where is he? Put him on,' implores Rajiv.

Rajiv can hear the woman burst into tears. He doesn't know how to react. He waits for her to say something.

'Emanuele is no more. My Emanuele is no more,' says Maria, barely able to put the words together.

Rajiv is stunned. 'When? When did this happen? I am so sorry, Maria. When?'

'Two weeks ago. Heart attack. He collapsed while catching fish in the morning,' says Maria.

'I am so sorry. I don't know what to say. He was a good friend. He was a good man,' says Rajiv.

'Thank you. He loved India,' replies Maria and then as an afterthought, adds, 'Strange. You are the second man from India within a week enquiring about him.'

'Oh, he had many Indian friends,' says Rajiv. 'I will miss him. If I can ask, who was the other Indian? Maybe I know him.'

'Some police inspector,' says Maria, a little unsure as she tries to recollect. 'From Mumbai. Yes, I remember his name now. Dayanand Apte. He rang five days ago, wanted to speak with Emanuele.'

A shiver runs down Rajiv's spine. Dayanand Apte. He says his goodbye to Maria and disconnects the phone. He returns to his bed and pulls the blanket over him. But he is wide awake. His eyes are locked on the wall clock opposite. His mind is running wild with thoughts. And the most troubling among them is, why would Apte want to contact Emanuele after the case has been closed?

* * *

'Finally we meet,' says Rupesh Kothari.

'A real pleasure, sir,' says Siddharth with a nervous smile. CEO of the Kothari-funded think tank Morpheus Research Foundation, Siddharth Patankar knows everything there is to know about telecom policy. He is seated across Rupesh and his personal secretary, Jagat Viramani, in the Kothari private jet. They are flying to Dubai for a meeting with the crown prince and a Chinese delegation.

Viramani hands Rupesh a memo Siddharth has prepared for the meeting. Rupesh flicks through it before placing it on the table. 'I'd much rather hear this from the horse's mouth.

So, Siddharth—I am told you have been with MRF since its inception?'

'Yes.'

'Great. And you are the telecom expert, they say?'

Siddharth smiles timidly.

'So, tell me,' says Rupesh, 'What are your views on the Chinese entering the 5G domain in India?'

'I am against it,' replies Siddharth. 'I am working on a paper on this very subject. It has been doing the rounds internally. In fact, the late Mr Mihir Kothari went through it and loved it.'

They don't have much time. They land in an hour, and the meeting with the crown prince is immediately after. 'Tell me the gist of it,' says Rupesh.

'Sure,' says Siddharth. 'In short, it would be disastrous for India to allow Chinese entry into 5G.'

'Disastrous is a strong word,' smiles Rupesh.

'Hardly,' says Siddharth. 'Mr Mihir Kothari concurred with my assessment.'

Rupesh is irritated by the constant reference to Mihir, but he holds back, not changing his expression. 'Our trade imbalance with China is 60 billion USD. Disastrous is always relative. But leave all that. Enlighten me on this 5G first.'

'5G,' begins Siddharth, 'or fifth-generation wireless communication is going to transform this century like no other technology. It will impact every sector—from our economy down to our cities and our security. The Chinese company Shangtel is one of the largest providers of 5G technology and equipment. But it is not merely a private company operating within the rules of Indian law to deliver services. Shangtel threatens our national security. China has laws that make it mandatory for Shangtel to gather secret intelligence in the nations that it operates from. That information is then promptly shared with the Chinese government. It follows that, any infra project a Chinese company is involved in here, China will know everything about it, sometimes even before our lawmakers do. This is the risk you should be aware of, more so because this risk is amplified in India's case due to China's open hostility towards India in most international forums, the long and disputed border the two countries share and China's closeness with Pakistan, a country that uses terror as a state policy against India. In fact, it is my view that no Chinese firm should be allowed into India's critical infrastructure, given that—'

'Thank you, Siddharth,' interrupts Rupesh with a wave of the hand. 'Now tell me, why is it dangerous?'

Siddharth clears his throat. 'While the benefits of 5G are unimaginable, those driving the technology can also wreak havoc on governments, citizens, financial flows and businesses at an unprecedented scale. To hand this infrastructure to a Chinese company bound by Chinese law to commit espionage is madness. Let me draw it out for you. Planes will fall from the sky, trains will crash, traffic signals will go haywire, phones will download wrong data, media will be manipulated—and all this will happen in a matter of minutes. Above all, imagine the possibility of injecting spyware into our financial systems or our stock markets. In border disputes and conflicts, or in support of Pakistan's terrorist activities, any or all of these would be tools in the hands of the Chinese government to destabilize India. No government can or should accept this level of risk for its people.'

'But Shangtel already has a major presence in India,' counters Rupesh.

Siddharth shakes his head. 'This is different. Shangtel's entry into the Indian 5G market is tantamount to India allowing Chinese State interference and—'

Rupesh stops Siddharth mid-flow. 'Correct me if I am wrong—Shangtel has stated time and again that it has no links to the Chinese state.'

'You are right, Mr Kothari,' says Siddharth. 'Shangtel has always denied any link with Chinese intelligence. It insists that it is a private company.'

'So then, what's with the scare-mongering?'

'America claims otherwise. It insists on China hiding the fact that it forces Shangtel to commit intellectual property theft in return for getting financed by the Chinese State. In 2019, Shangtel was indicted by the US Department of Justice and added to the "Entity List" of the US Department of Commerce.'

'Well, well, well,' smirks Rupesh, 'So the Yanks say Shangtel is dangerous. Of course they would. China is America's biggest challenger. Tell me something: is Shangtel the market leader in this domain?'

'Absolutely,' replies Siddharth. 'Shangtel has the highest number of 5G patents and makes the most technical contributions to the 5G standard. With 105 billion USD in revenues and 8.3 billion USD in net profits, Shangtel is not only the world's largest telecommunications equipment manufacturer, but also the world's largest telecommunications company across the value chain—from handhelds to networks. The company runs the telecom networks of the United Kingdom, Russia and 60 per cent of Europe.'

'Do you know who owns the largest private stake in Shangtel?' asks Rupesh.

Siddharth knows it is a rhetorical question. 'Yes,' he says, 'The crown prince.'

Rupesh smiles. 'Go on.'

'Shangtel's presence in India poses three major risks—from the Chinese State to our State, from the Chinese companies to our companies and finally from the Chinese citizens to our citizens. Please remember, not a leaf moves in China without Xi knowing about it. Here's the bottom line: all Chinese companies and individuals are bound by law to support China's intelligence agencies. This follows directly from the Chinese NIL, or National Intelligence Law. NIL applies to all Chinese companies, wherever they may be operating.'

Rupesh sniggers. 'Yes, yes, I get it. For you China is an enemy and the US a friend, Mr Patankar.'

'Yes sir, it is—just as it was for Mr Mihir Kothari.'

The Mihir reference yet again. Rupesh fidgets in his seat and gestures for Siddharth to proceed.

'While there is no doubt that economic interdependence has created an atmosphere of strained peace between India and China, the fact is that China continues to reman aggressive and looking for trouble.'

'Let's stick to 5G and leave foreign policy to others, shall we? India hasn't banned either Shangtel or any of its subsidiaries.'

'Yes, true. But it is also true that China is a surveillance state; it not only encourages espionage but demands it. Companies have little option but to fall in line. A recent Bloomberg report details how China managed to infiltrate some of the biggest American companies, from Apple to Amazon. In the case of India, the stakes are substantially higher. We have fought a war. Our nations function differently, our ideologies are polar opposite. China wants to harm us – on every front. And it will not think twice before asking its companies to fight this war.'

'How are we faring on the 5G indigenous front, then?'

'Of course, we are way behind China, although some baby steps are being taken. There are a few developments on this front though, largely led by IIT Madras. Amongst other things, they are working on developing MIMO or multiple-input multiple-output dense networks and wireless solutions especially tailored for India's present and future requirements, given the rapid pace of change in the financial sector.'

'Time to sum up,' says Rupesh.

Siddharth nods. 'Let me be blunt: India cannot afford to allow any Chinese presence in its tech and infra sectors. We must continue to frame policies assuming the worst about Beijing's intentions. We may not be going to war anytime soon, but the clouds are gathering. Besides, India will not be an outlier if it bans Shangtel. In India's favour is a rising nationalism under which not merely companies but also consumers and investors will shun any operator that uses Shangtel. As India becomes a larger economy and its disparity with China reduces, new opportunities will arise. Who knows?'

Rupesh raises his glass. 'Thank you, Siddharth. That was very informative. Who knows, indeed!'

Siddharth nods appreciatively.

Rupesh continues. 'But what I *do* know is the following. In an hour's time I will be signing an MoU with the crown prince as well as ratifying a secret understanding with China Telecom, vouched for by the crown prince.'

'About what, Mr Kothari?' asks Siddharth.

'China will allow unrestricted entry to Kothari telecom in China. And I will make sure that Shangtel gets into the Indian 5G space,' says Rupesh.

Siddharth is stunned.

Rupesh continues. 'And I also know one other thing. That this coming Saturday you will publish an article strongly advocating Shangtel's entry into the Indian 5G space. Then, together, we will meet the telecom minister and finalize all the paperwork for the Rajya Sabha Select Committee.'

Siddharth is struggling to speak. He feels dizzy. Gathering just enough strength to respond, he says, 'That, Mr Kothari, is impossible. I will never do that.'

'Oh, you will,' smiles Rupesh. 'Everyone has a price. What is yours?'

Siddharth looks at Rupesh with disdain. 'I just spent the last hour telling you why I am convinced of the opposite. Sorry. You don't know me.'

'Oh, you are quite correct on that count,' smiles Rupesh. 'I don't know you. Unfortunately, Jagat here does.'

On cue, Jagat Viramani clicks open a video clip on his phone and shows it to Siddharth. He increases the volume.

Siddharth's world collapses right before his eyes. He is trembling with rage, but more than that, with fear. He turns away.

Rupesh turns to Viramani. 'What did you say her name was?'

'Radha,' says Viramani.

Rupesh taps the table with his knuckles. 'Ah, yes. Radha. God, she does moan a lot, doesn't she. Don't think Mrs Patankar would mind seeing this clip. Not to mention newspapers and TV channels.'

'Stop,' pleads Siddharth. 'I'll do what you ask.'

'Good,' laughs Rupesh. 'And trust me. There are plenty more moans where those came from.'

Siddharth hides his face in his palm.

'And now, if you will excuse me,' says Rupesh, 'I have to go through the MoU draft one last time. By the way, Mr Patankar, here's a small token of our appreciation for all the work you do and how wonderfully you manage the MRF. It was nice meeting with you.' He hands him a box.

Siddharth gets up and leaves the table. He is still trembling and sweating as he staggers to the back of the plane. He collapses on his seat and stares at the box in his hand for a good minute.

He flicks open the lid. It is a Rolex.

* * *

8

Inspector Apte is in his study when the doorbell rings. It is just after dinner, and he has just left the company of his wife after having had his fill of the saas-bahu soap that he is coerced into watching with her every night. She barely notices him leave. Apte follows a set routine. He abandons the soap midway and goes to the kitchen to make himself tea that he takes to his study, where no one is allowed to enter except him. The study has been turned into an operation centre, a one-man task force. Flow charts, names of individuals and suspects, their photos and newspaper cuttings surround the centre table at which Apte sits and broods. He spends hours here; that's all he does after coming home from work. Tonight, he is going over his notes from the last day of the hearing when Rajiv's sentence was announced. He clicks his tongue, annoyed at the bell and shouts for his wife to answer the door. She shouts back that she is busy. Apte huffs and gets up to do it himself.

A man is standing at the entrance. It is Rajiv Mehra.

Apte recognizes him instantly despite the bushy beard. It is the eyes. The same set of eyes Apte has stared at so many times these past months. Rajiv's eyes have kindness in them, not guilt. This has always irked Apte. And now he stands before Rajiv, their gazes locked. No words are exchanged. Apte moves aside, allowing Rajiv to step in. His wife shouts from the living room, asking who is at the door. Apte shouts back an incoherent grunt and ushers Rajiv into his study. He gestures to Rajiv to take the lone chair while he leans against the panel on which the flow charts and photos are pinned. They once again stare at each other. No words pass through their lips for a good minute. The silence is becoming uncomfortable. Apte breaks it. 'What brings you to me?' he asks in his trademark cool, collected tone.

'I didn't kill Mihir,' says Rajiv. 'And I am here because you know I didn't kill him.'

'And what makes you think that?'

'Are you denying it?'

'I ask the questions, not you.'

'You contacted Emanuele—*after* the case was closed; *after* I was declared dead. Why?'

Apte is stunned, his thoughts in a frenzy, trying to figure out how Rajiv knows this. Rajiv doesn't wait for Apte to respond. He knows Apte has acceded. 'Inspector Apte, you know I didn't kill Mihir. You have known this all throughout, probably from the first day. Tell me I am wrong.'

Apte peels away from the panel and then falls back on it. 'I go by evidence. I believe what I see.'

'And what did you see—the fake receipts and letters from the Kotharis imputing to me a motive?'

Apte is silent for a few seconds. 'That's your conjecture,' he says, his voice unsure.

'Is it?'

'Yes. Did you dispute the evidence in court?'

Now it is Rajiv's turn to be silent. He collects himself. 'Look, Inspector. I am not here to confront you or accuse you. I am here to ask you to help me. I know you know I didn't kill Mihir. Help me.'

Apte is touched, but he maintains his characteristic poker face. 'I go by evidence, as I said. Can you dispute the fact that it was you who mixed cyanide in the soufflé? Is the CCTV footage lying? Can you dispute the fact that it was you who came out of your room in the evening, and that all your movements from that moment on are captured on CCTV? Can you dispute the fact that it was you who slashed your wrist and tried to hang yourself?'

'No, I can't,' says Rajiv, crestfallen. 'But I know something is not right. Or else why would you call Emanuele after the case has been closed?'

Apte sips his tea. The room is silent except for the ticking of the clock and Apte's slurps. He places the cup on the table, and as he does so, his expression changes. 'Rajiv,' he says, 'it is time to tell you the truth. Yes, something is not right about this case. There are inconsistencies. But I can't explain them.'

'Like?' asks Rajiv.

'Move over,' says Apte and unlocks the desktop screen. He pulls up the CCTV footage. 'Watch this,' he says, pointing a pencil at one of the panels. 'You entered the Maharaja suite at 11.35 a.m. and exited at 11.41. And then you exited it once again at 7.15 p.m. I can't explain how you entered the suite only once but exited twice.'

Rajiv is speechless. His jaw drops. He rakes his hair with a quivering hand. He looks at Apte with what can only be described as a grateful expression. There is relief on his face, immense relief. He knows now that Apte has figured out he isn't the killer.

'Wait,' says Apte as though he has read Rajiv's mind. 'Don't get ahead of yourself. Explain to me how this is possible.'

'Well, it isn't possible.'

'Was there another door or a passageway in the suite that the CCTV could not capture?'

'No, of course there isn't,' says Rajiv shaking his head. 'And you know it as well. You were there.'

'Then how? Look here.' Apte moves the screen capture of Rajiv exiting at 11.41 a.m. adjacent to the one of Rajiv exiting at 7.15 p.m. 'Isn't this you in both these screenshots?'

Rajiv leans forward and stares hard at the images. 'It is me,' he says finally, slumping back against the chair.

'There you go, then,' says Apte. 'I've been racking my brain for a week. How did you exit twice after entering only once?'

Rajiv covers his face with his palms in exasperation, then looks up at Apte. 'Is it possible that—?'

'What?' asks Apte.

'Is it possible that the person exiting at 7.15 p.m. is not me but someone impersonating me?'

'Well, that's a long shot when you yourself can't make out the difference between the man who exits and enters. Who will believe otherwise?'

'Wait,' implores Rajiv. 'What if the man exiting at 7.15 is wearing a mask?'

'Say that again?' says Apte, flabbergasted.

'You might find it ludicrous, but hyper-real masks are a reality.'

Apte looks at the ceiling and smirks. 'That's all I need right now.'

'You think I'm kidding? A year ago, someone impersonated the French defence minister by wearing a hyper-real latex mask. He managed to dupe even Aga Khan of millions. Technology has improved so much that one in three now cannot distinguish between the real face and its HRL impersonation. HRL masks are a world of sophistication away from their early *Mission Impossible* avatars.'

'Well, I don't know what to say. The images don't lie,' says Apte, looking at the computer screen. 'If it is indeed a mask, it's an amazingly good one. It's a masterpiece. Who would be able to make one this good?'

'Someone who knows every minute dimension of my face and skull, my every sweat pore and hair follicle.'

'And that'd be you,' sniggers Apte.

'Me. And Appleby,' says Rajiv.

'Who?'

'The principal expert at Magdeleine Tussauds.'

'Go on,' prods Apte.

'I don't know if you know, but there's a wax statue of me at Magdeleine Tussauds at London.'

'I didn't know that.'

'There is. And it took twenty sittings for Appleby to capture and replicate the profile of my face and head, every wrinkle of it, down to every strand of my hair, leave alone the shade.'

'Where are you going with this?' asks Apte.

'All I am saying is, if there is a possibility of someone impersonating me with a hyper-real mask, it has to be Appleby, no one else.'

'You have his number?'

'I used to. I don't remember it. But we can Google it.'

'Go ahead,' says Apte.

Rajiv opens the Google search window and types in 'Appleby Magdeleine Tussauds London'. The screen floods with images and links. 'That's him,' says Rajiv.

Apte comes closer to have a look. 'Call that Magdeleine Tussauds number.'

'I don't have a phone,' says Rajiv.

Apte gives Rajiv a dirty stare and dials the number. 'It must be nearing closing time there,' he says, as the phone rings at the other end. A male voice finally answers. Apte asks to be connected to Appleby. The voice turns glum. 'I am sorry, sir, but Mr Appleby is no more. He died in a house fire.'

'I am sorry to hear that. When did this happen?' asks Apte.

'Three weeks ago,' answers the voice. 'Can I help you with anything else?'

'No, thank you,' says Apte and disconnects. He looks at Rajiv. 'Appleby is dead.'

Rajiv is shocked. 'First Emanuele and now Appleby,' he says. 'You still think I killed Mihir?'

'Proof and evidence,' says Apte. 'I go by proof and evidence. If you *are* innocent, we would need to prove it. We would need to find out who the real killer is.'

Rajiv is comforted by the usage of the 'we'. 'Inspector Apte,' he says, 'I was not wrong in coming here to meet you. My hunch was right. Thank you.'

'There's nothing to thank,' says Apte, his annoyance building. 'We've got nothing by way of direct evidence.'

'But we have a start,' says Rajiv. 'We both know I didn't do it. We both know something is not right. What is to be our next step?'

Before Apte can answer, there's a knock at the door. He rushes to the door and opens it a little. It is his wife.

'I heard some noises,' she says and then ducks her head in, curious.

Apte swings the door open. 'Come in,' he says, 'I need to tell you something. This here is Rajiv Mehra.'

Rajiv turns around and gets up from the chair. Mrs Apte takes a step back, shocked. 'But wasn't he . . . wasn't he found dead?'

'Calm down, Rohini,' says Apte, patting his wife's shoulder. 'That was a lie, hatched by Mumbai Police's finest.'

Apte goes on to disclose to his wife whatever little he can get away with. 'Rajiv will be staying with us,' he says afterwards. 'You are to tell no one about this, absolutely no one. You hear me?'

Rohini nods. She steals a glance at Rajiv and then quickly averts her eyes.

'He will sleep here, in my study, for the time being,' adds Apte. 'And listen, Rohini. Look at me. I believe Rajiv is innocent.'

'But you yourself told the judge he was guilty,' replies Rohini.

'I did. But since then some evidence has surfaced that makes me doubt my assessment,' says Apte. 'But these are early days. We need to prove it. And we need to find out who really killed Mihir if it wasn't Rajiv. Keep everything normal. Just go about your life as you are. Rajiv will stay here until I can find him an alternative accommodation. He is safe here. Now just give me a minute. I'll join you upstairs.'

Rohini nods at Rajiv, a little unsure.

Once Apte and Rajiv are by themselves, Apte pulls out the sofa seat, turning it into a bed. He pats the mattress and throws in a blanket. 'Make yourself comfortable,' he tells

Rajiv. 'Use the flow charts and photos if you want. Tell me if anything comes to your mind.'

Rajiv nods.

'And do one thing,' says Apte. 'Go through the entire CCTV footage of that day. You can start tomorrow morning. Now rest. Don't leave the room or the house. Good night.'

Rajiv holds Apte's hand and squeezes it as a way of saying thank you.

'Later,' says Apte. 'We have just begun,' he adds before exiting the room, leaving Rajiv staring at the panel.

* * *

Sub Inspector Nair is chatting on the phone as he walks to his car in the underground car park at the Mumbai Police headquarters. He is in a jovial mood, relieved that his shift is over. He has been doing overtime for the past week because of a staff crunch. It is past midnight, and the car park is deserted except for a stray dog that Nair has disturbed with his loud talking. He gets into his car, lodges the phone between his cheek and shoulder and turns on the ignition. '*Haan milte hain sham ko*,' he says and disconnects. He switches on the music system. The sonorous voice of Kishore Kumar fills the cabin. Before Nair can put the car in gear, a steel wire is wrapped around his neck. Nair thrashes his arms and gasps, but the hold is strong. The man holding the wire from behind tightens it further. He is wearing a police uniform. He takes his right hand off and lodges a quarter bottle of rum inside Nair's mouth even as he gurgles and gasps for air. 'Why did you take the Taaj CD away?' asks the man.

Nair's face is turning purple, his eyes bulging. He still tries, futilely, to wrench away the wire.

'Tell me. Why did you take the CD away?' repeats the man.

A few seconds pass. The man eases his grip to allow Nair to speak. But he can't anymore. He sputters blood and is dead. The man shakes Nair, but he is gone. His body slumps forward and his head falls to his chest. The man sighs an expletive. He gets out from the back seat and climbs in the front after manoeuvring Nair on to the adjacent passenger seat. He lowers Nair's cap and adjusts his own. He puts the idling car into gear and drives off.

It takes him ten minutes to reach the deserted red-light district. He brings the car to a halt by the kerb, sprinkles some rum on Nair, tosses the bottle inside, and gets out of the car, gently closing the door behind him.

He checks his watch; it is 1.30 a.m. He lowers his arm and jiggles his wrist. The blue dial of his Rolex shimmers as it catches the light from the lone streetlamp.

* * *

There is a knock at the door. It is Rohini with some breakfast—poha and tea. Rajiv thanks her. They indulge in polite conversation.

'If you need anything, please let me know,' says Rohini.

'Will do,' nods Rajiv.

Rohini surveys the study. The bed has been converted back into a sofa. The curtains are drawn. She walks up to the window and slides it open. 'I don't know if my husband advised you to stay put inside this room,' she says, 'but you are welcome to come and watch TV in the living room. Or come to the kitchen for anything you want.'

'Thank you,' says Rajiv. 'I am very grateful.'

'You can teach me a few recipes as well, if you like,' grins Rohini.

Rajiv smiles back. 'Chances are you know more than I do in that department. Maharashtrian delicacies are my weak spot.'

'I'll make something Marathi for lunch then,' says Rohini.

'I'll look forward to it,' smiles Rajiv as Rohini takes her leave.

By forenoon, Rajiv's eyes are tired from staring relentlessly at the screen. He has been up since seven going through the CCTV feed. He isn't fast-forwarding the footage; he doesn't want to miss anything, any clue or moment that might be crucial. It has been a gruelling exercise, and he has reached only till the point where the hotel manager has welcomed him and shown him to the Maharaja suite. Rajiv takes a breather and sips at another cup of tea. He stretches his arms and gets back to screening the footage.

At lunchtime, Rohini asks Rajiv to lunch with her in the dining room. He obliges. The spread is typical Maharashtrian coastal cuisine. Rajiv is beyond impressed; he is envious, and he tells Rohini this. There is a relaxed air to their conversation, and it is comforting to Rajiv. This is the first time in months he is laughing and cheery while chatting with someone. It is a weight off his mind. They discuss food and friendships and relationships. Rohini even tells him the reason why she is so uninhibited with Rajiv. It is because Apte told her last night that Rajiv could not have killed Kothari. 'I believe him. And, therefore, I believe you,' she says.

'Thank you,' says Rajiv.

For Rohini too, having Rajiv around is a blessing. At least there is someone to talk to during the day. 'What would you like for dinner?' she asks.

'Oh, come on,' cries Rajiv. 'After this, how can anyone have dinner!'

They laugh heartily.

'You are married?' Rohini asks.

'No,' he says, 'I fell in love with someone who was married.'

Rohini tries to comfort him. 'That's sad. All your great creations, they are for people you don't love.'

'That's true in a way,' admits Rajiv, a little surprised by her perceptiveness.

Rohini smiles. 'Imagine how much more amazing your creations would be if you made them for someone you were madly in love with.'

This hits Rajiv like a bolt. 'You could be right. I never thought about it like that. You mean that extra bit of garnish missing from my dishes—it is love?'

'You could say that,' laughs Rohini. 'Did you ever cook anything for her, this woman you loved?'

Rajiv goes quiet. 'Once,' he says, after a while.

'What was it?'

'Soufflé,' blurts Rajiv and then regrets it.

Rohini ignores the parallel. 'And did she savour it before you two were in love?'

'Yes.'

'And was the second time better?'

'Oh, yes.'

Rajiv recollects Neelima's reaction to his soufflé. She had gone wild.

'Well, there you go.'

'Indeed. So, these incredible dishes you just cooked, Rohini—you mean they would have tasted even better had you—'

'Yes,' says Rohini before Rajiv can finish the sentence. 'Had I cooked them for Dayanand. But there's a catch.'

'Yes? What?' asks Rajiv, bemused.

Rohini smiles; her eyes exude honesty. 'They would have tasted best twenty years ago, when I was madly in love with him. Now I am just in love with him.'

'I see.'

'There are grades of love, aren't there? "Madly in love" changes to "being in love", as with a friend. Husbands become that after a while.'

'Hah, you could say that. I wouldn't know.'

'You mean, you still love her as madly as you did earlier?'

'Yes. But I don't discount what you say. Maybe if I were living with her, mad love, as you call it, would change into friendly love.'

'It doesn't change anything, though, does it? You'd still die for her, like I would for Daya.'

'Of course.'

There is a pause in the conversation. 'Time is getting on,' says Rajiv. 'I should get back to work.'

'Yes,' says Rohini. 'I will see you at dinner. But I dare say we won't have such free-flowing conversation at the table then.'

Rajiv laughs. 'He is a serious man, isn't he, your husband.'

Rohini sighs playfully. 'Half the things he says only with his eyes.'

'And the other half?'

'He doesn't say at all. Police habit, I suppose. It is as though he is always collecting information.'

Rajiv smiles. 'Thank you for this, Mrs Apte,' he says, getting up. 'I haven't had this much fun in months.'

'I know,' says Rohini. 'If you need anything just let me know.'

Back in the study, Rajiv resumes the arduous task of screening the footage. Afternoon turns to evening, but the curtains are still drawn. Rajiv has lost all sense of time. His eyes are tired and watery. He thinks of taking a break but every time he wants to, he says to himself, 'Just a few minutes more. Matters of life and death aren't resolved over tea breaks.'

And then, just as suddenly, it happens.

The footage is at the point where the man from housekeeping is pushing the trolley down the fourth-floor corridor towards the Maharaja suite—that sequence in the passage when he enters the suite and, a few minutes later, at 7.08 p.m. to be precise, someone who is impersonating Rajiv exits it.

Rajiv rewinds the footage to the moment when the man is rolling the trolley. And then it dawns on him. How did his lawyer and Apte miss it? Why didn't they wonder what happened to the housekeeping man and his trolley? Neither came out of the suite.

Rajiv is dumbfounded. A chill passes through his body. His head feels woozy. How could they miss this? He knows how. Because, focused as they were on Rajiv, they trawled the footage only for the portions that had him, so all their attention was on him exiting the room and then proceeding to the lift. No one thought of the housekeeping man who disappeared inside the suite and never emerged from it.

Rajiv freezes the frame and enlarges it. Only the back of the man is visible. He rolls the footage back and forth and pauses where the housekeeping man is swiping the card on the door lock to enter the suite. He zooms in on the image. He can see it clearly now. A watch with a radiant navy-blue dial. He has seen it before somewhere. But where? He stares hard at the frozen screen. 'Where?' he shouts out loud.

And then he remembers. He shoots up and rushes out of the room. He finds Rohini in the kitchen, preparing dinner.

'Can you please call Inspector Apte for me?' asks Rajiv, trying to hide his excitement.

'Sure,' says Rohini. 'He must be on his way,' she adds as she dials Apte's number and hands the phone to Rajiv.

Apte answers the call, thinking it is Rohini. 'What now? I am driving,' he says, irritated. 'I'll be home soon.'

'Inspector, this is Rajiv,' replies Rajiv with a smirk.

Apte's voice is embarrassed. 'Tell me,' he says.

'I think I know who the killer is.'

Apte presses on the brake pedal in reaction. 'Who?'

'I don't know his name. But we can find out,' says Rajiv.

'I'll be home in fifteen minutes. Let's talk then,' replies Apte and disconnects before Rajiv can say goodbye.

Rajiv hands the phone back to Rohini and returns to the study. Inside, settled on the chair, he stares at the wall clock and then at the desktop screen and then back at the clock. Fifteen minutes pass by. The doorbell rings. Apte is true to his word, says Rajiv to himself. He gets up impulsively to answer the door, but then remembers who he is and why he is hiding. It could be someone else. He sits back down again. A minute later there is a knock at the door. Apte enters. 'What do you have?' he asks without wasting a breath.

'How could you miss it?'

'Miss what?'

'How could you? I would have been acquitted.'

'What are you talking about?'

'*This*,' shouts Rajiv, pointing at the screen.

Apte turns to look. 'I still don't know what you are talking about. This is a blow-up of the housekeeping man about to enter your room. So?'

'So?' cries Rajiv. '*So?*'

'Enough fooling around. Tell me.'

'Look closely. The housekeeping man goes in.'

'Yes, he does.'

'But does he come out? Ever? What happens to him? He disappears!'

Apte staggers back, realizing the implications of this.

'You missed it,' cries Rajiv. 'You missed it, damn it. He never comes out. Instead, Rajiv comes out. Or the one all of you thought was Rajiv.'

'Oh my god,' stutters Apte. 'What have we done? I . . . I am sorry. What can I say. This is just . . .'

Rajiv calms down a little seeing how disturbed Apte is. 'I would have been hanged for this. A good thing the accident happened. You are saved from having a guilty conscience.'

Apte expresses remorse through his gestures. He sits down and exhales a sigh, thankful that Rajiv is taking it in his stride. 'This is terrible. I am ashamed. How could we miss this?'

'It's all right,' says Rajiv. 'Even my wretched lawyer missed this. All of you were focusing only on Rajiv. You missed tracking the housekeeping staff.'

Apte shakes his head in apology. 'So, what happened to him? We went through the entire footage. No one emerged from the suite except Rajiv—I mean the man impersonating you, and then us, of course, with the real you on the stretcher. What happened to the housekeeping man?'

Rajiv looks at Apte, but pauses for a moment before answering.

'He comes out.'

'When?'

'At 7.08. As Rajiv.'

Apte is astounded. 'Yes, it makes sense,' he says after having collected his breath. 'You said on the phone that you know who he is?'

'Yes. Look closely at the screen,' prods Rajiv.

Apte stares hard at the image. Nothing registers. He looks up at Rajiv.

'I have seen that blue dial before.'

'Where?'

'At a party. Two months ago. Rohan Kothari's wedding. In Phuket, Thailand. I saw the clip a month ago. This guy spilled wine on me. It's the same watch. Rolex.'

'You know his name?'

'No. He was a waiter at the party.'

'Can you recall his face?'

'That's the thing. I've been racking my brain over it. I am not sure. I think the video shows his face, but I am not sure.'

'Where's the video?'

Rajiv looks away. 'It was on my phone. I deleted it. In anger and sadness. I saw it on impulse while watching Mihir's funeral. I am sorry.'

'You remember who sent you the video?' asks Apte.

'Yes. Neelima did. She shot it.'

'So, it might still be on her phone?'

'Yes. And if it is there, we might catch the killer's face.'

Apte nods. 'Well, that leaves us no choice. Let me call her and ask her to come over.'

'What, now?' asks Rajiv surprised.

'Why, what are you waiting for?'

'No, nothing. Just. She will see me here. Or do you want me to hide from her?'

'No. We'll fill her in; tell her what we know. She trusts you.'

'She does.'

Rajiv stares blankly at Apte.

Apte brings out his trademark poker face. 'Let me call her. You have her number?'

'9810023489,' blurts out Rajiv.

Apte can't help but smile at how instinctive the answer was. Rajiv looks away, embarrassed. Apte dials the number. A woman answers the call.

'Hello, is this Mrs Neelima Kothari Thapar?'

'Yes?'

'I am Inspector Dayanand Apte. I was in charge of the Kothari murder case.'

A silence follows. 'Yes, I know,' says Neelima after a long pause.

'I would like to meet with you,' says Apte. 'I have come across some startling evidence that you might be interested in. Can we meet tonight?'

'What evidence?' asks Neelima.

'It is better that I tell you in person, Mrs Thapar,' replies Apte.

'Tonight?' repeats Neelima.

'Yes. I will WhatsApp you my home address and location. How soon can you come?'

'I can start in a few minutes.'

'Thank you. Looking forward,' says Apte and disconnects the call. He looks at Rajiv. 'She's coming over right away.'

An odd emotion sweeps over Rajiv. He doesn't know how to respond. Apte understands. 'Don't worry. I will do the talking. We can have dinner meanwhile,' he says and walks out of the study.

* * *

9

Krishan Thapar, cigar in mouth, strides over to the table where the Kotharis are seated and throws his helmet to the ground. 'Did you see that? Clear foul. The referee has had it, I swear.'

They are at the Amateur Riders' Club at the Mahalaxmi grounds, enjoying a leisurely Sunday afternoon. The sun is gentle and the breeze sluggish. 'Well, at least you survived with your limbs intact. I just don't know what you see in this game,' says Mihir.

'It is the game of kings,' says Krishan, blowing a smoke ring.

'We Kotharis like to play the game of kingmakers,' quips Neelima.

Krishan laughs gruffly and points to her with his cigar. 'Now that was a good one. Deserves a toast. Let me get changed. We'll go inside and grab a few drinks.'

The Kotharis watch Krishan leave. Their stares linger on the ungainly sight. Miraben is the first to comment. 'Neelima, what do you think?'

Neelima turns her head and stares at her mother. 'About what?'

'About him.'

'What is there to think, Ma? He is loud and brash and fat and lumpy and corrupt and laughs like an otter on helium.'

Mihir can't help but chuckle. Miraben admonishes him with a dirty stare and turns to Neelima. 'Enough with your silly jokes, Neelima. He is nice. He has taste. I think he'll be a great addition to the Kotharis,' she says.

'But Mihir is already married, Ma.'

'Quiet!' says Miraben. 'We are talking about you.'

'Keep talking, Ma. I am not listening.'

'Don't be like that. Physical appearances can change. A few hours at the gym every day—that's all it takes. Look, he is an interesting man. I see nothing wrong. I am going to offer him your hand in marriage.'

Neelima sputters. 'What? Are you crazy?'

'No. You are.' Miraben looks pointedly at Neelima's prosthetic leg.

'Don't be cheap, Ma. I am not a beggar.'

'Neelu. It's not like we have a line of prospective grooms waiting outside. You aren't getting younger. And I am getting older.'

Neelima turns to her brother. 'Mihir, tell her. Or are you going to stay mum like an obedient mama's boy?'

Miraben cuts in. 'Look Neelu. He's a great guy. I like him. Mihir likes him. And he doesn't mind the wooden leg.'

'Wow. So, you have talked to him already? This is low. Even by your standards.'

'I am your mother. I can't see my daughter stay single forever.'

'Well, marry me off to a tree then. Anything would be better than this ogre.'

'Neelu, listen. We need him. He is the only one who can swing the defence deal our way.'

'Ah. Now the mist clears.'

'Nothing like that, honey. That's not the primary reason, I hope you realize that. He also has no objection to marrying a disabled person.'

'Do you even think of me as your child, Ma? Or am I part of your business deals? I feel like throwing up. In his helmet.'

'He's going to save the Kotharis, Neelu. We need that government contract. We as a company are done for otherwise. You want me to beg you?'

Neelima is quiet. A tear forms at the corner of her eye. She looks at Mihir, but her brother looks away. 'I'd like to hear from my dear brother, what he has to say about Ma here selling me off.'

'That's disgusting, the way you put it.'

'Let Mihir open his mouth.'

But Mihir doesn't. He keeps looking into the distance. Neelima falls silent. She knows she is done for.

The silence is broken by Krishan's approaching cackle.

'The king returns,' he shouts. 'C'mon everyone, let's go inside,' he says, offering his hand to Neelima, who takes it, looking at her mother all the time.

'Oh. I almost forgot. This is for you,' says Krishan as he hands Neelima a polo ball. 'Signed by me.'

'Now I must learn how to play polo. So I can keep striking this,' says Neelima.

'This girl, I tell you, haan, Mihir?' says Krishan, throwing a playful punch at Neelima's upper arm.

'What are you going to toast to, Krishan?' asks Neelima tauntingly.

'To kings and kingmakers.'

'Nice,' says Neelima staring at Miraben. 'All together at one place. I'd give an arm and a leg for that.'

Krishan breaks into a loud laugh. 'You are good, you are. An arm and a leg.'

Neelima smiles. She ventures out of her chair slowly, looking at Mihir. 'An arm and a leg indeed.'

Neelima presses the brake pedal hard with her prosthetic leg, swerving to avoid the oncoming traffic. She comes to her senses and grips the steering wheel more firmly. 'Apte's home must be here somewhere,' she says to herself, looking out the window. The sudden braking has flipped open the glove box. Inside is the signed polo ball.

* * *

The doorbell rings while the Aptes and Rajiv are having their dinner. They look at one another.

'You want to answer the door?' Apte asks Rajiv.

'It's better that you do,' says Rajiv.

'All right then,' Apte tells Rajiv, 'You go to the study. We can talk there.' He turns to Rohini.

'Yes, yes, I know,' says Rohini, pre-empting him. 'I'll be upstairs.'

It is Neelima at the door. Apte welcomes her and ushers her into the study. Rajiv is at the desk. He turns around.

Neelima looks at him. She cries out and then staggers back, searching for support. 'No,' she exhales, cupping her mouth with her palm. Her eyes have welled up. Rajiv wants to kiss her, but he restrains himself.

Apte breaks the silence. 'Mrs Thapar, let me—'

'Call me Neelima, Inspector.'

'Yes. Neelima, please take a seat. I need to fill you in. Here is where we stand. I believe Rajiv is innocent.'

Neelima doesn't pay attention to what Apte has said. She is lost in her own thoughts.

'But how? You survived the accident?' she says to Rajiv, tears snaking down her cheeks. 'But they said, they said you were killed. They identified your body through DNA. My god.'

Rajiv exhales. There is a nervous half-smile on his face. 'Hello, N,' he says.

Apte butts in, forcing Neelima to look at him. 'It was a cover up. I believe, in fact, I am sure of it now, that Rajiv is innocent. Someone impersonated him at the Taaj that day. We have circumstantial proof of that. The person Rajiv spoke to last on that day is dead. The man who impersonated Rajiv did so wearing a hyper-real latex mask that he most probably acquired from a template at Madame Tussauds, London, which houses Rajiv's wax statue. The man who made the template is dead. There's more. From the CCTV footage of the Taaj that day, we know that it couldn't have been Rajiv who killed your brother. The man who did—here, see this image—wore a blue watch, a Rolex. He entered the suite and never emerged from it, only Rajiv did—I mean, the man impersonating Rajiv. This same man. You recognize him?'

Neelima stares at the screenshot. 'I can't see his face,' she says.

'Yes. I meant do you recognize the Rolex?'

'No. Sorry, Inspector.'

'Rajiv here thinks he does. He saw it in a clip you sent to him. A video you had shot during your niece's marriage celebration in Thailand.'

'I see.'

'Unfortunately, Rajiv cannot remember if this man's face was visible on that clip. And he has deleted it. We are hoping you may still have it.'

Neelima takes a moment to catch her breath. It's a lot to take in. She looks at Rajiv. Her eyes are filled with love. She wants to stride over and give him a bear hug.

'Let me check. I think I may still have it,' she tells Apte, and unlocking her phone, searches for the clip.

'Take your time,' says Apte.

'Is it this one?' asks Neelima after a minute, showing the phone to Rajiv.

'Yes,' says Rajiv.

Neelima plays the clip and hands the phone to Rajiv. Halfway through, Rajiv pauses the clip and zooms in. He shows the screen to Apte. 'It's the exact same dial. Rolex.'

Apte nods. Rajiv plays the clip again, till its completion. 'The man's face is not captured,' he says, downcast.

Apte turns to Neelima. 'Is there any other video of the wedding that you took?'

'Sorry, no. That's the only one. But it's possible to get to this man. The wedding reception, even though it was held at the James Bond Island, was arranged through a Phuket destination-wedding agency. My office arranged it, in fact.

I can get you the address and number of the agency. They should know about this man; perhaps he was from the catering agency. Someone needs to go to Thailand to investigate.'

Silence ensues. Apte breaks it. 'That will be me. I'll leave tomorrow. Please keep this to yourself. I'll tell Rohini that I am off to Aurangabad for some work.'

'I should come with you,' says Rajiv.

'*What*,' says Apte incredulously, 'With no passport and a persona non grata? No need. Besides, you won't be of much help there.'

Rajiv nods reluctantly. He walks up to Neelima and holds her hand, and then, with Apte watching, releases it.

Apte turns to Neelima. 'Thank you. You have been a great help.'

Neelima stretches her lips to fashion a thin smile. 'I am still in a daze, Inspector. But I can't thank god enough. Rajiv is alive. I always knew you were innocent,' she says, looking at Rajiv. 'But I had no proof.'

'No one did,' says Rajiv, 'Not the police, and not my lawyer.'

Apte addresses both Neelima and Rajiv. 'I must also tell you that this changes nothing for the time being. Rajiv must remain in hiding. Neelima, you mustn't contact him for the next few days. It is for his own good.'

Neelima nods gloomily.

'I better be off. Need to prepare for the trip,' says Apte.

Rajiv, overrun with emotions, gathers the nerve to hug Neelima lightly, knowing Apte is watching. They separate, and Apte escorts Neelima to the entrance.

'Keep me informed, Inspector,' says Neelima warmly as she bids him goodbye. 'And anything I can do, anything, please let me know. And it goes without saying that I will be sponsoring your Thailand trip and any other expenses incurred. My office will arrange everything right away.'

'Will do, and thank you,' says Apte and closes the door.

Apte enters the study without knocking. Rajiv is waiting for him. 'You should have married her,' he tells Rajiv, placing a hand on his shoulder.

'I will,' says Rajiv, 'Once I am proven innocent and brought back from the dead.'

'Leave that to me,' says Apte and walks out.

* * *

The wheels of Thai Airways flight TG2203 touch down on the rain-soaked runway of the Phuket International Airport. It is just past noon. Inspector Apte remembers to greet the guard at the arrivals with a Thai greeting. He gets a generous smile and a bow in return. The lounge is packed with tourists. He emerges from the airport and hires a cab to the Hyatt Regency. Neelima's office has made all the arrangements, including a ferry ride to Khao Phing Kan, or James Bond Island, where the Kothari marriage celebration took place. Apte dumps his suitcase at the hotel and after a quick shower is out again, to get to the destination-wedding agency in downtown Phuket. The bell desk informs him it is a brisk twenty-minute walk there.

Apte sets out on foot. The weather is pleasant and the street busy with cyclists. It is flanked on one side by picturesque detached and semi-detached houses and shops, and on the other by the ocean, from which a warm breeze blows landwards. He has to keep reminding himself he is here on business and not pleasure. He locates the agency without much trouble. It is in an old building, beautifully constructed in granite and wood, with 'Passion Wedding Planners' engraved in cursive on a plaque at the entrance. Long ceiling fans whir over a spacious hall inside. Apte walks up to the manager and introduces himself. The manager is polite and welcoming.

'What can I do for you?' he asks.

Apte takes out his phone. 'I am looking for someone. He was part of the staff you provided for a wedding celebration at James Bond Island two months ago,' he says and plays the video on his phone. The manager watches the clip intently, taking off his glasses.

'Oh yes, I remember,' he says. He replaces his glasses. 'A wonderful wedding. Went all night long. The whole island had been hired by the family.'

'You have a list of the staff?'

'Yes. There were forty of them.'

'No, not the cooks and others. Just the waiters.'

'Ten, then.'

'Do you have their photographs and addresses?'

'Yes. One moment. We don't have any permanent hires. They come and go as per work.'

'I see. Can I have a look at the names and addresses, please?'

'Here,' says the manager, handing Apte a sheaf of papers. Apte skims through the forms. They carry the photographs and addresses of the hired hands. Three of them have Indian names—two men and one woman. 'Can I get a photocopy of these forms, please?' he asks, and then remembers the age he is in. 'Sorry. Can I click a photo of them?'

'Go ahead,' nods the manager.

Apte clicks photos of the ten forms. He zooms into the Indian faces and crops them into separate images. 'Thank you very much. You have been a great help,' he says, shaking the manager's hand.

It has started to drizzle. Apte decides to check out the woman first. Aditi Tyagi. He takes a tuk-tuk to her address, a small flat in a high-rise on the outskirts of Phuket town. Her apartment is on the fourth floor. He rings the bell. A woman with a baby straddling her waist answers it.

Apte bows politely. 'Are you Ms Aditi Tyagi?'

'Yes,' answers the woman guardedly. The baby begins to cry.

'I am Inspector Apte from Mumbai Police. Can I come in?'

'What's wrong? What happened?'

'Nothing. Just some routine questioning.'

Aditi swings the door open to let Apte in. 'Come in.'

'Thank you. We are making some enquiries regarding a marriage celebration hosted at the James Bond Island two months ago. You were hired by Passion Wedding Planners for the day.'

'Oh, yes, I remember. The Kotharis it was, wasn't it?'

'Yes. Do you know this man?' Apte plays the clip.

Aditi comes closer and tilts her head to watch the clip. 'Yes, I do. Amit Sansanwal. I think that was his name.'

Apte checks the forms. 'This person?'

'Yes. He was one of only two other Indians. The other was Dhruv Something. I forget his surname.'

'Dhruv Saha. This one?'

'Yes.'

'Can you tell me about him?'

'Who, Dhruv? Quiet person. He has a—'

'No. The other man. Amit Sansanwal.'

'Oh, okay. Nice. Friendly. Said he had come from India to find work in Thailand. Tall and handsome. I haven't seen him since that day.'

Apte calls the number listed on Sansanwal's form. No one picks up the phone. 'Can you tell me where this address is?' he asks Aditi.

'This is actually a motel, not far from here. Fifteen minutes by cab.'

'Thank you. I should get going.'

'Is anything the matter, Inspector? Has something happened to Amit?'

'No. Just routine enquiries,' says Apte and exits Aditi's apartment. Outside, he signals for a cab to stop and gets in. It has started to rain heavily now. The car wipers are swishing at full speed. Apte curses under his breath—so much for the promised good weather.

The motel, which opens on to a beach, is deserted. Apte gets out of the cab and runs into the lobby to save himself from the downpour. The hall is shabbily kept. The sofa on the side is worn and sprouting a spring.

He rings the desk bell. A man appears, bearing a disinterested look. Apte shows him Amit's photo. 'Is this man staying here?'

'Who are you?'

'I am Inspector Apte from Mumbai Police, India.'

The manager's demeanour turns respectful. He edges closer to have a better look. 'Yes, he was staying here a month ago. But he left.'

'Any idea where he might have gone?'

'No. He didn't leave a forwarding address for his mail, if that's what you are asking.'

'For how long did he stay at your motel?'

'A month. He paid upfront.'

'Cash?'

'Yes.'

Apte is disappointed. He thanks the manager and leaves.

It has stopped raining by the time Apte gets back to his hotel. Truth be told, he is pleased with the progress he has made. He might learn more when he visits James Bond Island tomorrow. There is a possibility the man he is looking for is working there. Apte calls up room service for a simple dinner and switches on the TV. He takes a shower and returns to ring up his wife.

'How's everything at home?' he asks Rohini, skipping the greetings.

'Fine,' comes the curt, but soft reply. 'How's Aurangabad?'

'Fine. I'll be returning in a couple of days. Is Rajiv there?'

'He must be in his room.'

'Call him and put him on the phone. I want to talk to him.'

Apte senses irritation at the other end. He smiles to himself.

'Okay, wait,' says Rohini. 'Let me go to the study.'

'Waiting,' says Apte, still smiling to himself.

The doorbell rings. It is room service. Apte opens the door and turns around, the phone to his ear, waiting for Rajiv to come on. He walks a few steps to the TV table. 'C'mon, what's taking you so—,' he mutters. But he can't finish the sentence. A shimmering blade swishes clean across his throat. It happens in a flash. There is no time to react. Blood spurts and drenches the TV. Apte collapses as though in slow motion, first on his knees and then, as they buckle, flat on the ground. The phone falls from his grasp and bounces away on the carpet.

The man standing over the writhing Apte waits a moment or two. He wipes the knife with Apte's shirt, slowly, and replaces it in the sheath. Apte lies on the carpet, his eyes open, his throat slit clean. He gurgles a few words and then he is dead. A few feet away, Rajiv can be heard on the phone shouting hello repeatedly. The man steps over Apte's dead body and picks up the phone. He disconnects the call. He scrolls through the WhatsApp feed open on the screen. It is empty. There are only two chats, one of Apte with his wife, and the other with Neelima. Apte had sent her a message earlier in the day, intimating her that he had reached Phuket. The man combs through Apte's photos next. There are a dozen odd images that have been taken today. Ten of them are of forms. Three are photos. One is of the man currently staring at the phone. He smirks. He selects the photo of the other man, Dhruv Saha, and sends it to Neelima with the accompanying message: '*Found him!*' He switches off Apte's phone and wipes it clean. Then, folding back the cloth covering the room service trolley, he takes out his backpack and gets down to work.

* * *

Neelima and Rajiv are lying supine on the wet green grass of the rainswept Inner Hebrides cliff. The soles of their feet are touching, as they face the skies, eyes closed. Raindrops splatter on their faces, the wind howls. They are drenched to the bone. Neelima buckles her left knee; her foot detaches from Rajiv's. Rajiv cranes his neck and looks at Neelima.

'It is the real one,' she says.

'But I can still feel the sensation from the prosthetic,' he replies.

They laugh and get up and walk to their car hand in hand, with Neelima resting her head on Rajiv's shoulder.

They are driving back to London. This trip to Scotland was made on an impulse. They both wanted to get away from the crowds and work and friends and everything else that ties one down to the world.

'Can't we stay here longer?' she asks.

He doesn't respond. She looks at him with so much love in her eyes. Love and sadness. 'Can't we settle here? Just me and you.'

Neelima flops her feet on the dashboard in front and crosses her legs. She pushes the button on the music player. Her favourite song, 'Time to Say Goodbye' by Bocelli and Brightman, is playing.

> When I am alone I sit and dream
> And when I dream the words are missing
> Yes, I know that in a room so full of light
> That all the light is missing
> But I don't see you with me, with me
> Close up the windows, bring the sun to my room
> Through the door you've opened
> Close inside of me the light you see
> That you met in the darkness
> Time to say goodbye

Rajiv turns his head and looks into Neelima's eyes. He remains silent.

'Say something,' she implores, rubbing the back of his hand. He doesn't.

Horizons are never far
Would I have to find them alone?
Without true light of my own with you
I will go on ships overseas
That I now know
No, they don't exist anymore
It's time to say goodbye

'*Suno*,' she says. He looks at her. 'Will you marry me?' He looks away, back at the road. They are quiet for the next few minutes. It feels like an eternity for both.

When you were so far away
I sat alone and dreamt of the horizon
Then I know that you are here with me
Building bridges over land and sea
Shine a blinding light for you and me
To see, for us to be
It's time to say goodbye

'Neelima,' he says finally, 'you know I can't. You know we can't.'

'Don't speak for me,' cries Neelima, switching the music off in disgust. 'I can. You can't. You are a coward. All men are.'

Rajiv is outraged. 'Must you ruin this precious outing?'

'Coward.'

'It has been the best day of my life.'

'Coward.'

'The first of many. Hundreds of such days. Thousands.'

'Coward.'

Rajiv wants to say something but holds back.

'Who are you afraid of, Rajiv—Krishan? Mihir?'

'No one.'

'Mihir. What has he promised you? A chain of restaurants?'

'You are being cheap now, Neelima.'

'I can promise you a hundred restaurants.'

'Please stop.'

'And Krishan and his defence deals, and my mother and my brother grovelling before him . . .'

'Neelima . . .'

'They think I am a piece of wood. Sculpted wood.'

'Stop. Please . . .'

'A leg. I am a leg. Fuck them. And fuck you.'

'That's enough, Neelima, for heaven's sake—'

But it is too late. Before Rajiv can react, Neelima unbuckles her seatbelt, swings open the passenger door and jumps out of the moving car. Rajiv screams and applies the brakes. The airbags puff out in a flash. Squeezing them aside, he lunges out of the car. Neelima is lying on the road a few metres away. Rajiv runs to her and lifts her in his arms and brings her back to the car. She is moaning but putting up a brave face.

'That's the good thing about the leg,' she says. 'It doesn't hurt.'

Rajiv gently removes a few damp strands of hair from her forehead. A speeding lorry drives past, its shrill horn piercing his ears.

* * *

The shrillness of the doorbell wakes Rajiv with a start. He is sweating and panting. He rubs his eyes with his palm and stares at the wall clock. 9 a.m. He hasn't stepped out of the study since dinner last night, not even for a stroll down to the living room. He hears the main door being opened by Rohini and a polite hello and welcome. A minute passes by. There is a knock at the door. Rajiv gets up from the bed and goes to open it. It is Neelima. Behind her is Rohini, who leaves the two of them alone.

'This is a surprise,' says Rajiv. 'I was just—' he adds and then checks himself.

'I need to show you something,' says Neelima. 'You don't have a phone, and I didn't want to message Rohini this.'

Rajiv comes closer. Neelima shows him the WhatsApp message from Apte.

'This is the guy?' asks Rajiv. 'So Apte found him.'

'I have been trying to contact Apte since I got this message yesterday evening, but his phone is switched off.'

'Yes. Even we tried yesterday. He rang Rohini and asked her to put me on the phone. By the time I came on, the line went dead.'

'I don't like it. I don't like it at all.'

'Yes. He should have called. Or at least messaged you again. Did you check with the hotel?

'Yes. I rang them last night and then again this morning. They said no one is picking up the phone in the room.'

'Wasn't he supposed to go to James Bond Island today?'

'That's the thing. The manager said the cab waited for him early in the morning. And then left.'

'Something is not right.'

'And the manager was positive Apte didn't leave the hotel this morning. But when housekeeping entered his room, it was empty.'

'So he is not in the hotel. But he didn't take the cab in the morning. Did he slip out last night?'

'Rajiv, I am worried. If Apte found the killer, the killer could have found him, too. He has always been one step ahead.'

'Yes, no doubt about that.'

'I need to go to Phuket and find out. I must.'

'Don't be crazy, Neelima.'

'It's the only thing to do. We can't notify either the Thai police or the Indian authorities here. It will only unravel everything and complicate matters. For a start, they will land up here, and it won't take them long to find you out.'

'True. But—'

'Look. The police will want to know why Apte went to Phuket, when he told his wife he was off to Aurangabad.'

'Yes.'

'And in Phuket, who was he trying to catch, and why?'

'I agree. We can't involve the police at either end. So look, Neelima. I'll go.'

'Are you mad? You are in hiding, for god's sake.'

'Precisely the reason. No one knows I am alive. No one suspects anything. Your going would only raise eyebrows.'

'But—'

'Not buts. I have to. We cannot inform the police as you rightly pointed out. And of course, spare a thought for Rohini. She thinks Apte is in Aurangabad and returning day after tomorrow. How quickly can you arrange this for me, N?'

'I can take care of it by late afternoon. You can take the late-night flight to Phuket. It has a brief stopover at Bangkok.'

'The passport . . . ?'

'Don't worry. I know Krishan's contacts. At least knowing him can finally be of some help.'

The painful memories of abandoned promises sweep over them both. There is no point apologizing. Rajiv looks away. 'Thanks,' he says.

'I'll be back by four in the afternoon. Rajiv?'

'Yes?'

'No, nothing.'

'Tell me.'

'You take care of yourself. I don't like this.'

Rajiv takes Neelima's hand and holds it between his palms. 'I should have died a month ago. I was prepared for it, expecting it. If there is one thing now that I don't care about, it is my life. But I care about Apte's. And yours.'

Neelima's eyes well up. 'You will need a phone. I'll get one when I come with the passport.'

'No, don't. I won't carry a phone. I don't want to be tracked. The next you will hear from me is when I am back here, with Apte.'

'I don't have a good feeling about this, Rajiv.'

'Nothing will happen,' Rajiv comforts her. 'I will be back with Apte by tomorrow night. Promise. Now go. But before you do, take my photo. For the passport.'

Rajiv stands next to the wall and looks straight ahead, into Neelima's phone. She wants desperately to say 'smile' but resists. She clicks the photo. 'I'll be back,' she says.

'I'll wait,' he replies.

* * *

The shovel strikes the earth. He pushes its edge in with his foot and twists the handle. Taking a shovelful of dirt, he tosses it over the edge of the trench he stands inside of. Crickets chirp all around. He wipes the sweat off his brow and resumes digging. The sun is at its zenith. The field is deserted. He is well hidden by tall grass that sways this way and that in the breeze.

When the trench is deep enough, he jumps out and walks to his car. He opens the boot and pulls out Apte's body and drags it to the trench. Placing it next to the edge, he pushes the corpse in with his foot. He crushes Apte's mobile with the heel of his shoe and kicks it into the ditch, then starts to fill the ditch up with earth again.

* * *

IO

Vicky Gonzalez. That's who Rajiv is. He's wearing a Hawaiian shirt and chinos. A rucksack slung on his shoulders and a Rasta cap on his head completes his backpacker look. He gets through the Mumbai immigration and security without a hitch, but attracts a hippie in the waiting lounge. The man is from Southampton and has been backpacking his way through Asia for what appears to be much of his adult life. They get talking. It's a challenge for Rajiv, but he manages to concoct an entirely new version of his life's story. That's the thing about being dead—you are at liberty to invent your past. The rest of the journey is uneventful.

At Phuket Airport, Rajiv decides to change tack. He anticipates that he'll be watched by the assassin from the moment he lands at Phuket, so rather than take a cab to the Hyatt, he buys a cheap suit and discards his gruff backpacker look. He waits for his moment, and then mingles with a clutch of businessmen exiting the airport. Once out, he strides over to the bus terminal and takes a ride to downtown Phuket, confident that he has shrugged off any tail. He has a plan, and the first stop is the Passion Wedding Agency. He only has a photo of the killer to go by, the one sent by Apte to Neelima. No name or address. Rajiv locates the agency and after a friendly chat with the surprised manager, extracts the forms Apte had photographed and stored in his phone. He identifies Dhruv straight away. The address is provided in the form; it is at the other end of the city, the manager informs him. Rajiv sets out on the double.

It is a rundown quarter of Phuket. The streets are crowded with hawkers and vegetable sellers. Rajiv locates the address, but decides to first make enquiries from Dhruv Saha's neighbour. It turns out Dhruv has been in hospital for a good month. He suffered multiple injuries in a car accident, including a skull fracture. Rajiv thanks the neighbour and decides to go to the hospital. If what the neighbour says is indeed true, Dhruv could not be the assassin.

The Vachira Phuket Hospital is teeming with people. There is no security to talk of; the doctors and nurses seem least bothered. Relatives are mingling freely with the patients. Rajiv locates the general ward. He recognizes Dhruv by his photo. He is recuperating on a bed shrouded on three sides by a thin, moth-eaten curtain. His head is heavily bandaged, and his arm is pierced with needles. Numerous tubes and contraptions criss-cross his body like highways.

Rajiv walks up to him and drags a chair to the bed and sits down. He introduces himself as a friend of a waiter who was at the marriage celebration of the Kotharis. They get talking. Dhruv is forthcoming. He tells Rajiv of the horrid car accident that nearly took his life. He has been in the hospital for five weeks now, the first was spent in an induced coma.

'Can you tell me anything about Aditi Tyagi and Amit Sansanwal?' asks Rajiv. He shows him their photos.

The question clearly surprises Dhruv. 'Yes, I knew them,' says Dhruv. 'We worked together only once. Amit and I. With Aditi I have worked many times, not only in and around Phuket but we've gone to Bangkok as well for a wedding.'

'Tell me more about Amit.'

'As I said, I worked with him just once, for this. Never saw him after that. Maybe he stayed back on the island.'

'The address he gave is of a motel in Phuket.'

Dhruv looks at the form. 'Not far from here.'

'Did you talk much that day? The day of the wedding?'

'Hardly. He appeared to me to be the brooding type. Kept to himself.'

'Thanks. You have been a great help. I hope you recover soon.'

Dhruv nods and slides back on his bed. This chat was a relief. Rajiv has been the first visitor he has had since his accident.

At the motel, Rajiv hears the same story as Apte. Except this time, the manager demands cash in return for information. Coming out of the motel, Rajiv mulls his next step. It is obvious. He has to visit James Bond Island. There is every chance he might get to know more about Amit there; perhaps even bump into him. The island is secluded, far removed from habitation, but easy to connect to the rest of the world when he wants to. An ideal hideout.

Dawn is breaking as Rajiv speeds towards James Bond Island on a hired motorboat. It has been a tough night of hardly any sleep. The bunk beds of the YMCA made sure of that. Rajiv was up and running as soon as boats could be hired.

The person ferrying him is an old man, a practised hand, and not one to dispense the thrill of speed on water to his customers. The wide panorama of the sea as the sun comes up is spectacular. The sky is as blue as the waters and were it not for the orange hue of daybreak, it is difficult to tell where the sea ends and the sky begins. Soon, James Bond Island comes into view. It is a marvel of nature. Rajiv is in awe of what lies in front of him. Seagulls caw overhead as they approach the island, the noise from their motorboat dimming the sound of the ocean. All of a sudden, out of nowhere, a boat comes hurtling towards them. Both Rajiv and the old man have no time to react. All they can do is turn their heads in horror. Rajiv instinctively jumps into the sea a moment before the impact, but the old man cannot. As the two boats collide, the impact is catastrophic. Rajiv's boat breaks into two with an earth-shattering noise, its hull destroyed in a matter of seconds, debris flying everywhere.

The motorboat loops back to inspect the damage. The old man's dead body is floating in the sea along with wooden planks of the now destroyed boat. The man operating the motorboat switches off the engine and approaches the crash scene. But Rajiv is nowhere to be seen. The only dead body that has surfaced is that of the old man. A minute passes. The man in the motorboat takes out his gun and surveys the debris, hunting for any sign of Rajiv. As he crouches for a better look, Rajiv leaps on to the motorboat from behind and lunges at the man. The boat sways and rocks, about to capsize. There is a mad fight for control and a shower of fisticuffs. The assassin has recovered his composure and is now matching Rajiv blow for blow. The hand-to-hand combat is making the boat unsteady yet again and the next moment both Rajiv and the assassin topple over into the sea. They continue to grapple with each other under water. There is a mad scramble for the gun. Rajiv tries to snatch it but fails. The assassin sees his moment and fires, narrowly missing Rajiv's shoulder. Rajiv catches hold of the assassin's leg and pulls it, unsteadying the assassin. His body sweeps a tumbling circle. The gun releases from his grip. Rajiv lunges forward and grabs it as it sinks.

He aims at the assassin and fires two rounds. The bullets hit their mark. Blood gushes out and colours the water. Rajiv grabs the assassin by the collar and swims up. He can hardly hold air in his lungs anymore. Bubbles are escaping from his lips. But he manages to emerge into the open. He gasps for air hungrily, swallowing in mouthfuls. He has the wounded assassin by the collar, and he heaves him on to the motorboat. Then he climbs aboard.

There is silence all around for miles. The debris floats along with the old man's body, gently colliding with the motorboat and then moving away. The vast expanse of the sea is all there is. James Bond Island is in sight, its bewitching greenery a stunning contrast to the blue of the sea and the sky.

Propping himself against the side of the motorboat, Rajiv stares at the now dead assassin for a good minute. Then he gets up and inspects the assassin's pockets. He finds a mobile phone. It is locked. Rajiv opens it using the assassin's index finger. He scrolls through the contents—the messages, the WhatsApp calls and texts. There are photos of Rajiv by the dozens, and of Appleby, Emanuele, Nair and Apte. The photos have all been sent to one number, without an ID. Rajiv cannot recognize the number but is certain it is of the assassin's handler. The assassin, who used the name Amit Sansanwal, has not disclosed his real name in any message or text.

Rajiv takes a close-up selfie of his own battered, bloodied and swollen face—eyes closed—and sends it to the handler, with the message, '*Done.*' He removes all security features from the phone, including the screen lock's fingerprint requirements. Scrolling through the image gallery, one photo makes Rajiv startle and take note. It is of Rupesh Kothari. He is offering a toast with a raised glass. There is a broad grin on his face. Standing next to him is the crown prince. On the other side of Rupesh is a man—his arm slung around Rupesh's shoulder—who has, it is obvious, taken this selfie with his other hand. That man is lying dead in front of Rajiv.

* * *

'Mr Gonzales, would you like a drink before your dinner?'

Rajiv, his head leaning on the window, is gazing blankly at the clouds outside. It takes a few seconds for him to collect his wits and respond to the air hostess. 'No, thank you,' he tells her.

The late-night Thai Airways flight back to Mumbai is nearly empty, with a smattering of middle-aged Indians returning from their Bangkok escape. Rajiv has been trying to process the events that have unfolded in the last few days. He is exhausted and in pain; he is certain he has a few cracked ribs and a sprained ankle for good measure, and at the end of it all he doesn't know for sure the identity of the handler, nor does he have any proof against the mastermind who planned the spate of murders, beginning with that of Mihir Kothari. He is unsure of his next step; unsure whether he will ever be able to get rid of his new life, all the hiding and the anonymity; unsure how he will face Rohini. He peels away from the window in revulsion and switches on the LCD screen in front of him to distract himself, flicking through the channels, to finally settle on some news. The clip is of this morning, an event organized by the Kothari Group and Shangtel. Rupesh Kothari is seated on the dais next to the CEO of the Chinese company, along with the minister of telecommunications and the leader of the Opposition. Also present is the crown prince of Dubai. The large banner behind celebrates 'India-China Strategic Telecommunications Partnership for a Glorious Future'. The minister lights the lamp; the Chinese counterpart supports the Indian minister's hand from underneath as is the custom. Rupesh takes the stage. For the next five minutes he waxes eloquent on the benefits of the telecom partnership he has entered into, of how his brother had always wanted this and worked so hard to make it happen, of the tremendous opportunity the opening up of the China market has now given both India and the Kothari Group and how Shangtel entering the 5G space in India is a win-win for both countries. The audience applauds at every deliberate pause Rupesh makes. 'A momentous day,' he exults at the end. Rajiv switches off the screen and returns to cloud gazing.

Rajiv passes through Mumbai immigration without any hassle, then takes a cab to Colaba, to the Kothari office complex where Neelima will be at this morning hour. He has worked out in his mind how best to cushion her shock when he apprises her of the sordid developments.

At the office complex, Rajiv waits in the lobby for the opportune moment. He knows Reema, Neelima's secretary, comes down for a cigarette and coffee break at noon sharp. They have been good friends. He doesn't have to wait long.

He spots Reema striding towards the exit with coffee in her hand. He accosts her. She nearly faints.

'I will explain everything but not now,' he tells her.

She is speechless.

'I need a favour,' he continues.

She nods.

'Take me to Neelima. She is expecting me,' says Rajiv. Reema, still in shock, nods again and escorts Rajiv to the seventh floor. Neelima's office is at the end of the long corridor. Rajiv walks up to it and knocks on the glass door. Neelima is looking out the window. She swivels around. A gasp escapes her. Her expression is of shock and bewilderment. She stutters but manages to take Rajiv's name on the second attempt. 'You could have warned me you were coming,' she says, before returning to a staid expression.

'I didn't carry a phone as you know, N,' replies Rajiv. 'Also, there are things I couldn't have told you over the phone, at the risk of getting tracked.'

'I am so relieved to see you. Where's Apte? You dropped him home? Sit, sit. You want some coffee?'

'Later.'

'Tell me everything. Wait. Weren't you supposed to come by this morning's flight? And your face! Oh my god, Rajiv. What happened?'

'I decided to take the flight back last night itself. Listen, N. I will explain everything in detail but later. I need to do a few things right now.'

'Like what?'

'Apte is dead.'

'What? When? How?'

'It's awful. I don't know how to break it to Rohini. He was murdered.'

'Oh my god. By whom? When?'

'An assassin. A hired hand. The same guy in your video clip. The waiter.'

'Oh god.'

'He came after me, too. Tried to kill me. But I was lucky. I killed him, instead.'

Neelima's face bears a shocked expression. 'All this is— I don't know what to say, Rajiv. All this happened yesterday?'

'Yes. This man has a handler. In India. And I know who this handler is.'

'Who?'

'I am sorry, N. I know this will come as a shock to you, and that is why I came here first, as soon as I landed. I haven't even gone to Rohini and informed her of the tragedy.'

'Tell me.'

'It's your brother. Rupesh Kothari. I am sorry, N.'

'What?! Are you mad, Rajiv? Do you have any idea what you are saying?'

'I do.'

'You mean . . . you mean to say Rupesh got Mihir killed?'

'That's what I am saying, N.'

'But why? That's crazy.'

'Yes, it is crazy. But I want you to think about it. We need to dig for more proof. Join the dots. Make the connections. See the motive.'

'I . . . I don't know what to say, Rajiv.'

'Do you trust me, N?'

'Of course I do.'

'Then do as I say. I need to go now. I need to meet Rohini. And it's not safe for me to be exposed like this. I took a chance, not very clever of me. I'll see you in the evening. Let's meet at Rohini's. She'll be comforted to see you.'

'Sure. Sure. I'll come over in the evening.'

Rajiv is about to leave when Neelima strides over and holds his hand and then caresses his forehead and cheek. 'Gosh, it's all swollen, your eye. You must be in awful pain. At least this forehead wound looks to be an improvement from yesterday; it is healing.'

'Oh, it's nothing. I'm fine, N.'

'Take care, Rajiv.'

Rajiv says his goodbye and hurries out of Neelima's office. He walks to the elevator lobby and presses the lift button. The lift arrives, empty. Rajiv gets in and presses the button for the ground floor. He waits, staring at his reflection in the mirror opposite. Abruptly he remembers something.

The blood drains from his face. His eyes grow terror-struck. It is as though the floor has collapsed from right under his feet. He frantically presses the stop button and then presses for the seventh floor. When the lift arrives at the seventh, he rushes out and starts to run but slows to a brisk walk when people stare at him from either side of the corridor. He reaches Neelima's office. She cannot see him, but he can see her. Her face, as usual, is turned towards the window, and she is looking out. Rajiv takes out the assassin's phone and calls the handler's number. A second or two go by. And then it happens. The silence of Neelima's office is broken by a ringtone. It is coming not from the table where her phone can be seen, but from her handbag hung on the coat rack in the corner. Neelima swings her head towards the bag. And then she realizes what is happening; what the ringing means.

She shoots up out of her chair and in that moment sees Rajiv at the door. He has a phone held up. The rings continue, as shrill and upsetting as before. Rajiv takes a step in, stares at Neelima, and says, 'Aren't you going to pick it up?'

Neelima is speechless.

'Pick up the phone, Neelima,' dares Rajiv.

Neelima doesn't know how to react. She simply stares at Rajiv even as the ringing continues, sounding strangely louder and ominous. Rajiv takes a few steps in and drags up a chair. The ringing finally stops. 'You want me to call you again?' he asks.

Neelima parts her lips but swallows the words she is intending to utter. Her face is ashen.

'I am waiting, N,' insists Rajiv.

The silence is crushing. Neelima finally breaks it. 'How— how did you know?' she asks, almost in a whisper.

'My forehead wound—when you touched it and concluded it was healing. How could you have noticed the difference unless you'd seen the wound before? And you had. In that selfie I sent the handler from the assassin's phone.'

Neelima is silent. She squeezes her eyes shut and then opens them.

'Why did you do it, Neelima? Why did you kill your brother?'

'I didn't kill him.'

'Well, you'll have to do a lot better than that. At the police station. In court.'

'You . . . you don't understand. It was a mistake. A horrible mistake. He wasn't supposed to die.'

'Oh yes? Then who was?'

'The initials . . . '

'What?'

'The monogrammed soufflé plate—the initials. MK. That cyanide-laced soufflé wasn't meant for Mihir Kothari.'

'Then who? MK is . . . '

Rajiv freezes mid-sentence. 'Oh my god. Miraben Kothari? Your mother?'

Neelima averts her eyes. 'The soufflé plates got switched by the server. It was an accident. I loved Mihir.'

Rajiv shakes his head in disgust. 'You wanted your own mother dead?'

Neelima firms up for the first time. There is a sudden resolve in her voice. 'If your own mother sold you off for a few crumbs, you'd have wanted her dead, too. Don't go preachy on me. She is a monster.'

'No one's going preachy on you. Least of all I, who you condemned to rot inside a jail and die a dog's death.'

Neelima smirks. 'And what did you condemn me to? Love? Happiness? What were you afraid of? Cowards don't count.'

'And who decides that? You?'

'Yes. I decide. Me. Condemned by god who maimed me; condemned by my mother who sold me; condemned by my lover who spurned me. I decide.'

'I feel sorry for you. I loved you.'

'Save that crap for someone else, Rajiv. You never loved me. No one did. But I am not playing the victim here, crying buckets over it. Everyone gets what he or she deserves. And everyone is forgotten in the end. No one cares; nothing matters.'

'No, *you* save that crap for someone else. You are a murderer, Neelima. You murdered not just Mihir, but so many others. You murdered Apte. You planned to send him to Thailand, didn't you? And you planned to send me to Thailand as well. You were intimating the assassin of our plans and movements all throughout. And we walked right into it. No one would have known. No one would have guessed. It was a perfect plan.'

Neelima is stoic for a moment, and then, as though compelled by nature, lets her sardonic side come through. 'The Rolex ruined it, though.'

'Funny you can smirk even now. Nothing matters to you. Yet you mattered to me. And to think you were planning all this; to think I was a pawn for you.'

'What else are you? What else am I? We are all pawns to be sacrificed. Don't feel cheated. Take it in your stride.'

'Oh absolutely, N. Take it in my stride. You destroyed my life. I am dead for the world. You snatched from me my name, fame, friends, my life, everything. And you have the cheek to tell me to take it in my stride.'

'What else can you do?'

'Well, we'll see about that.'

Rajiv takes out the assassin's phone. Neelima can sense what he is about to do. She laughs. 'Go right ahead, Rajiv. And what will you tell the police? That I am the murderer and that you are innocent? That I killed my own brother? That I killed Apte?'

'I have the proof.'

'And what is it? The assassin's phone? And his messages to some handler who doesn't have a name?'

'You. You are the handler.'

'What makes you say so—this burner phone?' Neelima picks up the phone and wipes her fingerprints off it, smiling.

'There you go. Take it,' she says, tossing it in Rajiv's lap. 'Now what proof do you have against me?'

Rajiv is stunned. He tries to think quickly, but he can't come up with anything. He puts on a brave face.

'I am waiting,' says Neelima, coolness and poise personified. 'What proof do you have against me, Rajiv? What are you going to tell the police? Think; think quickly. What are you going to tell them? How are you going to connect me to all this?

'In fact, if at all, it is you who is going to be implicated. For Apte's murder to begin with. You went all the way to Thailand to get to him. Such was your drive to wipe out all evidence, to prevent Apte from getting to the truth. You killed him and buried him. And then you came for me.'

Rajiv's face drains of colour and he grabs the armrest in anger. But he knows Neelima is speaking the truth. He has nothing on her. And now, with her burner phone resting in his lap, even less so. He finds he is paralysed. He cannot speak or utter a word. He disconnects the call to the police.

Neelima gets up calmly and smiles. 'But I'll tell you what the police will think,' she says, picking up the swivel chair and throwing it against the window in one swift motion, her strength surprising Rajiv. The glass shatters into a million pieces. She walks up to the window, then turns around to face Rajiv. 'I will tell you what the police will think. They will think you killed Mihir and Apte, and you—'

Neelima hops on to the ledge. The wind is fierce. Her hair is all over the place. She has to shout out her words against the howling wind. 'They will think that you tried to kill me as well.'

Rajiv tries to spring up, but he can't move. He tries again.

Neelima holds on to the opposite sides of the window frame with her hands, as though she is parting them with force. The Vitruvian woman. 'But because I loved you, I'll do this for you. Give you a handicap, pun not intended. You have five minutes to run. I don't know if I will survive this, and if I do, we might meet again, but if I don't, I want you to know that I don't want you implicated in my murder. I give you five minutes to run. Run for your life. Bye Rajiv.'

Rajiv screams in horror and lunges to catch hold of Neelima, but it is too late. A smile on her face, she has toppled herself off the ledge. There is silence in the room. Rajiv is hypnotized, frozen. He can hear the silence pounding in his ears. And then comes the dull thwack. It is like a detonation in his head. Rajiv dare not look out. He dare not imagine. He turns around. He can hear the commotion down below, on the street. People are shouting and screaming. But in the office, it is strangely quiet. With Neelima's office at the very end of the corridor, no one has heard anything; no one has seen what just happened.

Rajiv knows what he has to do. He runs.

* * *

Acknowledgements

The author wishes to thank Milee Ashwarya, Shreya Mukherjee and Dipanjali Chadha for their expert editing and timely suggestions; Raveena Tandon for being there as a friend and for her constant encouragement; and Gautam Chikermane for helping draft one of the chapters sourced heavily from his brilliant essay on making a case for denying the Chinese entry into the Indian 5G domain.